Ken Ludwig's

Be My Baby

A SAMUEL FRENCH ACTING EDITION

FOUNDED 1830

NEW YORK HOLLYWOOD LONDON TORONTO

SAMUELFRENCH.COM

MUSIC USE NOTE

IMPORTANT BILLING AND CREDIT REQUIREMENTS

BE MY BABY had it's world premiere at the Alley Theatre, Gregory Boyd, Artistic Director; Terrence Dwyer, Managing Director, on September 30, 2005. The Scenic Designer was Alexander Dodge, the Costume Designer was David C. Woolard, the Lighting Designer was Donald Holder and the Sound Designer was John Gromada. The Production Stage Manager was Terry Cranshaw and the Stage Manager was Richard Constabile. The production was under the direction of John Rando with the following cast:

GLORIA NANCE	Elizabeth Bunch
MAUD KINCH	Dixie Carter
CHRISTY McCALL	Ty Mayberry
JOHN CAMPBELL	Hal Holbrook
MALE ENSEMBLE	James Black
FEMALE ENSEMBLE	Robin Moseley

CHARACTERS

JOHN CAMPBELL

MAUD KINCH

CHRISTY MCCALL

GLORIA NANCE

All other parts played by two actors, a man and a woman.

For my brother Gene,
who has always been my guiding light.

ACT I

(In the darkness, we hear the Ronettes' hit song "Be My Baby" coming through the sound system.
The lights come up and two women are riding in the front seat of a car on a bumpy road. The younger woman, GLORIA NANCE, is 19 years old. She's English, rich, vivacious and very sure of herself. She's the one driving. The other woman, in the passenger seat, is her aunt, MAUD KINCH. She's English, in her 50's and rather behind the times. At the moment, she's extremely unhappy. They're driving along a back road outside Aberdeen, Scotland, and the road is full of holes. The time is 1963. The music transfers loudly to the car radio.)

GLORIA. *(Over the noise of the song.)* We're almost there. We must be…

MAUD. *What?!*

GLORIA. I said we're almost there!

MAUD. *Would you turn that thing down for heaven's sake!* *(GLORIA turns down the radio.)* Honestly…Now what did you say?

GLORIA. I said we're almost at the house and it should be any...*Wait!* There's the barn! Do you see it?! Through the trees! ... Aunt Maud?!

MAUD. Yes?

GLORIA. *(Ecstatically) Do you see the barn?!*

MAUD. *(Blankly)*... Stunning. A miraculous barn.

GLORIA. It's Christy's, you know. And he owns all the land between here and the main house. And they named a whole village after his family. Over three hundred years ago. Oh, I love Scotland, don't you?

MAUD. It's very quaint.

GLORIA. And Christy is a real honest-to-God lord up here. I mean, he's nobility!

MAUD. I'm aware of that.

GLORIA. Oh, Maud, why do you hate him so much?

MAUD. What a thing to say.

GLORIA. You know you do. And it's unfair!

MAUD. *(Boiling)* I'm unfair. I'm unfair?! You completely disregard my advice! You make a mockery of my position. I made a promise to your parents before they died that I would take good care of you, and yet you force me into a position that makes a joke of my responsibility! *My authority!*

GLORIA. But he's wonderful!

MAUD. You are nineteen years old. You haven't the faintest idea what is wonderful and what is not wonderful. You should have waited to get engaged. I blame both of you.

GLORIA. In most societies, the woman is married when she reaches the age of fertility.

MAUD. How educational.

GLORIA. Aborigine women have all had intercourse by the time they're thirteen. Have I shocked you by saying that?

MAUD. Tremendously.

GLORIA. In some tribes, they actually celebrate the breaking of the woman's hy —

MAUD. *(Cutting her off.)* Let's *not* discuss it.

GLORIA. Oh, Maud, don't be a prune! I want you to love Christy as much as I do. And don't you simply adore John? He practically raised Christy, single-handed. Christy was orphaned even before I was. Did you know that?

MAUD. Of course I did.

GLORIA. John was their sort of house manager or something.

MAUD. Yes, I kn —

GLORIA. John is such a stone-face. But it's all show. He just takes some getting used to, that's all.

MAUD. *(With intense dislike.)* That is the understatement of the century. John Campbell is the rudest man that ever walked this earth.

GLORIA. Well *I* like him. I think he's funny.

MAUD. I'm sure you do. And I'm sure you'll be very happy living here — in the wilderness.

GLORIA. I'm sick of London.

MAUD. In my opinion, that is so ty —

GLORIA. *(Suddenly)* Oh, Maud, there's the house! Isn't it gorgeous! Oh, I wish you were getting married, too! It's so exciting! You will live with us? You promised.

MAUD. I said I would think about it.

GLORIA. *(Distressed)* But you *have* to! We'll be so happy together!

MAUD. We shall see.

GLORIA. Oh, Maud, I can't live without you. It's impossible. Please say yes. *Please!*

MAUD. Well, I –
GLORIA. *Look! There he is! It's Christy!*
MAUD. Wait until the car stops.
GLORIA. *Christy!*
MAUD. *The car! Mind the car!*

(MAUD is thrown around like a rag doll, as GLORIA screeches to a halt.)

GLORIA. *(Jumping out of the car before it completely stops.) Christy, we're here!*

(As GLORIA jumps out of the car, we see CHRISTY McCALL and JOHN CAMPBELL. CHRISTY is about 25, good-looking and likeable. He's Scots. JOHN is in his 60s, very matter-of-fact and unsmiling. Very Scots. Both men speak with a Scots accent, but JOHN'S is more marked. GLORIA runs to CHRISTY and throws her arms around him.)

CHRISTY. *Gloria!*
GLORIA. *Oh, Christy!*

(They kiss furiously. They're bursting with sexuality, and their lips and hands are all over each other. MAUD gets out of the car, swaying from the near-disaster. She nods to JOHN. They clearly don't like each other in the least.)

JOHN. Miss Kinch.
MAUD. Mr. Campbell.
JOHN. Welcome to Scotland.
MAUD. Thank you.

JOHN. …They're far too young to get married, you know.

MAUD. I'm very well aware of that.

JOHN. "Wisdom cries out in the streets and no man regards it."

MAUD. I agree entirely.

(This entire time, CHRISTY has been kissing GLORIA'S neck and ears, and GLORIA has been getting more and more excited. Now she jumps up and throws her legs around CHRISTY'S waist and their petting gets even more intense. They're virtually having sex in front of JOHN and MAUD.)

JOHN. However, I think we'd better set a date for the wedding before a child appears from spontaneous combustion.

(The lights fade and then come up on the kitchen in the main house, a few days later. It's the kind of kitchen that had a staff of five in the 19th century. Now it's run by MRS. ADAMS, who is bustling about preparing dinner. Maud ENTERS.)

MAUD. It smells absolutely divine in this kitchen. It reminds one of London.

(A GARDENER ENTERS, wheeling a barrow and unceremoniously plunks his morning's bounty on the cook's table.)

GARDENER. Turnips. *(Thud)* Onions. *(Thud)* Cabbage. *(Thud)* Beets. *(Thud)*…And two coneys. *(Thud. As he EXITS, he tips his hat to MAUD.)* Ma'am…

(He EXITS.)

MAUD. ... Yes, it smells divine.

MRS. ADAMS. *(Pleased)* Thank you, mum. It's the apple dumplings.

MAUD. Dumplings! You're joking! My mother and I used to make apple dumplings together at our home in London, on the Edgeware Road. It was such a remarkable place to grow up.

MRS. ADAMS. I've never been to London, mum.

MAUD. *(Incredulous)* Never?

MRS. ADAMS. I always intended to.

MAUD. Then you must come and visit me. On your next holiday. I insist, that's final.

MRS. ADAMS. Oh, mum —

MAUD. I don't want to hear any arguments, it is completely settled. *(Beat)* If I go back at all. I'm not sure that I can bear to leave Gloria.

MRS. ADAMS. I know just how you feel, mum. I have two girls meself. But there comes a time when you have to let 'em fly on their own. Even if they take off arse backwards.

(John ENTERS in his shirtsleeves. He sees MAUD and stops short — then enters the room anyway.)

JOHN. 'Evening.

MAUD. *(Acidly)* Good evening. Now as I was saying, Mrs. Adams, in my opinion, if one is tired of London, one is tired of life.

JOHN. I believe that Samuel Johnson had the same opinion about two hundred years ago.

MAUD. Really? What an amazing coincidence. *(Looking into one of the pots.)* Ah! Now what is this? The smell is heaven!

MRS. ADAMS. That'll be the haggis, mum. We'll be havin' that at the weddin'.

MAUD. Do you know, I've heard about haggis since I was a child. I love that word. "Haggis." Now what is that white thing bobbing around there in the water? It looks fascinating.

MRS. ADAMS. That'd be the guts, mum. [She pronounces it "goots," to rhyme with "foot's."]

MAUD. I beg your pardon?

MRS. ADAMS. The guts. The stomach. O' the sheep. You can do it with calf guts, but most of us think that sheep is better.

JOHN. I'tis better. It's got more juice.

MAUD. *(Horrified)* You're serving a...a...sheep's stomach at my niece's wedding?

JOHN. *(With a laugh at her ignorance.)* Nay, o' course not. 'Tis only boiled in the stomach. The sweetness is in the chopped heart and lungs.

MAUD. Oh!

MRS. ADAMS. It's very popular.

MAUD. No. I'm sorry, but I'm afraid not. I won't have it.

JOHN. ... You "won't have it"?

MAUD. No. Sorry.

JOHN. *(Restraining himself.)* I'm obliged to tell you, madam, it is not a question of your havin' or not havin'.

MAUD. But we have guests coming from *London!*

JOHN. Let 'em come from Timbuktu — !

MAUD. They'll be *disgusted!*

JOHN. *(Roaring) Then let 'em go home with my compliments!*

MAUD. ... I will speak to Christy about it.

JOHN. You can speak to Jesus Christ Almighty and his Apostles and it'll make no difference! And I'll thank you not to be stickin' your nose into everything else appertainin' to this household!

MAUD. *(Quivering with indignation.)* In my opinion, you are a very rude man, and I pity you. I have half a mind to leave here today and *never come back.*

JOHN. What would it take to convince the other half?!

(JOHN stomps out of the kitchen. He strides across the back lawn of the house, where he's joined by CHRISTY.)

CHRISTY. John! Please!

JOHN. No!

CHRISTY. Please! Just listen!

JOHN. *No!*

CHRISTY. But you know what it means to me!

JOHN. I would not hurt you for the world, boy, but I will not attend the wedding if that she-devil is there.

CHRISTY. Now wait. She didn't really do anything -

JOHN. Everything is wrong accordin' to her. First it was the seating arrangements. Then the time of the wedding. Now it's the haggis. I'm surprised she hasn't asked for a Mooslim ceremony!

CHRISTY. John —

JOHN. *(Mimicking MAUD'S voice.)* "In my opinion..." Everything is "in my opinion." If I hear that one more time I'll stuff her tongue up her nose.

CHRISTY. Look —

JOHN. *She objected to the kilts, for God's sake!*

CHRISTY. She'll only be here for another month! That's the plan, anyway.

JOHN. *(Aghast)* A month? The wedding is Saturday. She could be out o' here by Sunday noon.

CHRISTY. We can't just tell her to leave that quickly.

JOHN. Why not?

CHRISTY. She's Gloria's aunt! You can't do that to Gloria. She's had no one else in the world since she was a child. She'd be heartbroken.

JOHN. The next thing you know, she'll be wantin' to live here.

(Beat. CHRISTY avoids his eyes.)

CHRISTY. Well ...

JOHN. Oh dear God.

CHRISTY. John —

JOHN. Say it's not true.

CHRISTY. It's been discussed. That's all. It's very unlikely.

JOHN. "Unlikely?"

CHRISTY. Now listen —

JOHN. Ya must be mad!

CHRISTY. Just listen! *(A deep breath, then he plunges ahead.)* First of all...now hear me out...I-I've agreed about the kilts. There'll be no kilts at the wedding. *(Silence)* Maud asked for an English wedding, and I agreed to that, from the start. I gave my word. So nobody's wearing kilts. It's black tie. Sorry.

(JOHN, tight-lipped, walks out of the room.)

CHRISTY. John...*John! Hey! I'm not finished! (Running after him.) We got to pick the church, didn't we?!*

(As the lights fade, wedding bells start pealing. The lights come up on MAUD and GLORIA in GLORIA'S bedroom. MAUD is sitting with GLORIA'S wedding dress in her lap. She's trying to repair it with a needle and thread, getting more and more anxious by the second. GLORIA, in her slip, is pacing nervously.)

MAUD. *(Cross)* Just look at this dress. It's a wreck.

GLORIA. Maud, we only have ten minutes.

MAUD. Well it cannot be repaired properly in ten minutes! The entire lining is ripped. Despite what you think, I am not Hercules. How you could possibly tear the lining of a brand new wedding dress that has never been worn outside this room, I will never know.

GLORIA. I wore it downstairs this morning, to show Christy.

(MAUD stops cold and gapes at GLORIA.)

MAUD. ... You didn't.

GLORIA. I wanted him to see it. I guess I was excited.

MAUD. *(Distressed, working herself into a state.)* Gloria! How *could* you! It's bad luck for the groom to see the gown before the wedding! Even *you* know that!

GLORIA. Oh, Maud —

MAUD. It is the worst possible thing you can do!

GLORIA. That's an old wives' tale, and you know it —

MAUD. We *must* get you a new gown!
GLORIA. Maud!
MAUD. But there isn't *time!*
GLORIA. Maud!!
MAUD. Oh, what should we *do*?!
GLORIA. Maud, stop it —
MAUD. *(Distraught)* Oh, Gloria, how could you *do* this?! How could you possibly be so terribly, terribly *thoughtless*—!
GLORIA. *(Flaring with anger.)* MAUD, STOP IT RIGHT NOW! JUST FIX THE DRESS!

(Silence. MAUD turns away, hurt. GLORIA instantly repents.)

GLORIA. Oh, Maud, I'm sorry, I'm sorry. *(She kneels next to MAUD and hugs her.)* I don't know what's wrong with me.

(MAUD strokes her hair.)

MAUD. You're getting married. And you're a little frightened. It's perfectly natural. I'm sure I'd feel exactly the same way. *(Beat)* Now I've got to finish. *(She goes back to the dress.)* And I still don't understand how you did this. It's ripped right up the bodice. The only way that could happen is if you tore it off as fast as you could, without even thinking. Just ripped it off in a state of ...

(She suddenly realizes how it must have happened. She looks at GLORIA, and GLORIA giggles. MAUD buries herself back into her work.)

MAUD. ...I don't want to talk about it. I have just lost interest in the entire conversation.

(The lights cross-fade, so we now see JOHN and CHRISTY in CHRISTY'S bedroom.)

CHRISTY. Help me with the tie here.
JOHN. Aye …

(As he ties CHRISTY'S tie:)

GLORIA. Oh Aunt Maud, I'm sorry – but I couldn't help myself.
MAUD. Of course you could. To be civilized is to be restrained. Find limits to your behavior.
GLORIA. For you it is. Because you're so much older than everybody else.
MAUD. It is called experience.
JOHN. *(Finishing the tie.)* There.
MAUD. *(Finishing the dress.)* There.
JOHN. Quite respectable. And don't tell me *that's* too tight.
CHRISTY. John. You don't think I'm making a mistake, do you?
JOHN. Dreadful mistake. But that's marriage for you.
GLORIA. You don't want me to live alone all my life, do you?
MAUD. Of course not. But that doesn't mean handing out everything in advance.
CHRISTY. I mean Gloria. You do like her, don't you?
JOHN. Do you like her?
CHRISTY. I don't think I can live without her.
JOHN. Then you'd be a fool not to marry her, wouldn't you.
MRS. ADAMS. *(Hurrying in.)* Mr. Campbell, sir?! You'd

better hurry! The congregation is gettin' restless. And Parson McNair excused himself to the gents and he came back smellin' o' whiskey!

JOHN. We'll be right there.

(MRS. ADAMS EXITS. CHRISTY takes a deep breath.)

CHRISTY. Wish me luck.

JOHN. You don't need luck, my lad. *(Christy exits.)* I'm the one who needs the luck.

(As he walks out the door and disappears, lights come up in the church. The wedding is about to begin, and we hear the noise of the congregation. PARSON McNAIR is waiting impatiently at the pulpit. He looks at his watch.)

PARSON MCNAIR. Come on, come on, I ain't got all day. You'd think it was the marriage o' David and Bathsheba. Or Liz Taylor. *(Calling off.) I got a baptism at two o'clock, and the little tyke ain't gonna be happy! (Back to the congregation.)* I hope they ain't back there havin' premarital sex or somethin'. While we're waitin', let me remind you that we've now sold 32 tickets to the Annual Loch Mull Dinner Dance and Fly Fishin' Competition. I've done me math, and that represents 75 percent o' the population so keep up the good work. Also, the Sunday School picnic has been postponed for lack of interest. ...Ah. Here we go. It's about time.

(CHRISTY hurries in and stands to one side of the pulpit. Then he sees MAUD sitting in the first row. He hurries over and gives her a kiss on the cheek.)

MAUD. Good luck, dear boy. Please take care of her.

CHRISTY. I will, Aunt Maud. I promise.

(CHRISTY goes back to where he was. He nods to MCNAIR, who nods to the organist. The introductory chords ring out, followed by "Here Comes the Bride." GLORIA AP-PEARS at the back of the church in her wedding gown. She looks gorgeous. She holds out her arm, and John appears; he's giving her away.
But JOHN is now wearing a kilt.)

GLORIA. *(Whispering fiercely.)* John! What's that?! That's a kilt!
   JOHN. That's because we're in Scotland, me lassie. And so is this: *(He calls out loudly.) Open the doors, gentlemen, and play your hearts out!*

(The doors of the church are thrown open, and we hear "Here Comes the Bride" being played by an army of bagpipers. The whine of the bagpipes drowns out the organ. MAUD turns around in her chair, in a state of shock. CHRISTY shakes his head. And JOHN walks proudly up the aisle with GLORIA on his arm.
When he and MAUD sit down in their pews, on opposite sides of the stage, he gives his kilt a shake – and flashes her. She recoils in horror – and the lights fade quickly.
They then come up on a room in the main house. It's night, and the room is empty. We hear heavy rain and possibly thunder outside. Then we hear MAUD'S voice calling in the distance.)

MAUD. *(Off)* Hello?!...Hello-o?! *(After a moment, MAUD*

hurries in, pulling her coat off, soaking wet. She looks highly distressed.) Christy?!

(No answer. Then MRS. ADAMS ENTERS.)

MAUD. *Mrs. Adams! How is she?! How's Gloria?!*

MRS. ADAMS. The doctor is in with her now, along with Christy and Mr. Campbell. I know they're doing all they can.

MAUD. I would have been here sooner, but the train was delayed. Unaccountably! It just *sat* there, in the station, for over an hour, *not moving at all,* and…I should have been here!

MRS. ADAMS. There's nothing anyone could have done. It just happened all of a sudden. Without any warning. She was perfectly fine all day, and no one suspected a thing. Not a single thing.

MAUD. *I* would have suspected. *I* would have known.

MRS. ADAMS. He's a very good doctor, Miss Kinch. Of that I promise you. He delivered all my children – every one of them – and I'm sure he's doing everything that he possibly can. And I've said a prayer, and so has all the staff …

(JOHN ENTERS, in trousers and shirt sleeves, looking weary and upset.)

MAUD. Mr. Campbell. How is she?! How's my Gloria?!

JOHN. The doctor is still somewhat concerned.

MAUD. Oh, no.

JOHN. They were at a party, but of course the baby isn't due for six weeks. She had a sort of…spasm, and we brought her back here, thinkin' it was no great shakes. Now they don't want to move her.

MAUD. Oh dear God. Where is she?

JOHN. Upstairs, but I think you should wait. Christy's in with her.

MAUD. I want to see her *right now!*

JOHN. I know you do.

MAUD. *(Losing control.)* I should have been here. It's my fault. I didn't *need* to visit London. It was vanity, that's all it was. Sheer vanity.

JOHN. It would have happened anyway.

MAUD. She's all I've got.

JOHN. I know.

MAUD. *(Starting to cry.)* I feel so helpless.

JOHN. I suppose God must have a higher purpose in mind with all this. But for the life o' me I can't figure out what it is.

MAUD. *(Fiercely, bitterly.)* I don't believe that for one... millionth of a second. Higher purpose. If anything happens to that girl, I will never have faith in anything. Ever.

JOHN. It's all a great mystery. I suppose if it wasn't, every preacher on earth would be hanged by now.

(CHRISTY ENTERS, looking pale. They stare at him without breathing.)

CHRISTY. Gloria's all right. She'll be fine.

MAUD. Oh, thank God! Can I see her now? *(CHRISTY nods, and MAUD rushes out of the room.)* Gloria!

(She's gone. JOHN sees from CHRISTY'S expression that something is wrong.)

JOHN. But?

CHRISTY. ... The baby was stillborn. ...The doctor says, because of the...damage, she can't have any more children.

(CHRISTY cries and JOHN holds him. The lights fade. They then come up in the gardens behind the house. CHRISTY is alone, sitting on a stone fence, thinking, when GLORIA hurries in, waving a letter.)

GLORIA. Christy!...Christy, look!

CHRISTY. Gloria, would you stay in bed!

GLORIA. *Look!* It's a letter from Celia!

CHRISTY. Celia?

GLORIA. *(Sighs with disgust.)* My cousin from San Francisco. She was at the wedding. Don't you remember anything?

CHRISTY. I was nervous.

GLORIA. The pretty one. Blonde. She wore the teal dress with the spaghetti straps and the hideous blue pumps.

CHRISTY. With the glasses.

GLORIA. That was Annabel!

CHRISTY. Oh.

GLORIA. God. Men are so stupid. Now listen. Celia and Tim have been having problems.

CHRISTY. Tim?

GLORIA. Her husband! Dark. Tall. Long arms.

CHRISTY. Swings from trees.

GLORIA. You could see there was trouble brewing at the reception. He was eyeing everything in a skirt. It was disgusting. Well, Celia got pregnant right after that, God knows how, and she had the baby last week, a little girl, but now they're getting a divorce.

CHRISTY. Ooh, bad timing.

GLORIA. No, it's *perfect* timing. They're putting the baby up for adoption.

CHRISTY. Why?

GLORIA. Oh they both say they want their "freedom." Celia was always a pea-brain. If she didn't have that incredible figure she'd be totally useless.

CHRISTY. Oh, *Celia.*

GLORIA. Christy, I want the baby. I want to adopt her. Don't you see, it's perfect! She's a newborn. In perfect health. They're getting a divorce and they'll just hand her over to an agency or something. *It's perfect.*

CHRISTY. We'll have to think about this.

GLORIA. There isn't *time* to think about it! We'll lose our chance! If they give her to an agency, she'll be gone. Christy, I want to call them right now. And I want to go to San Francisco.

CHRISTY. Gloria! You're *not* even supposed to be out of bed!

GLORIA. I'm fine.

CHRISTY. No you're *not* fine. The doctor would have a fit.

GLORIA. I don't care! Christy, it's fate. It has to be. Please. *Please.*

CHRISTY. ... I guess I could go myself.

GLORIA. *No!* You'd be useless by yourself. Taking care of a baby?

CHRISTY. Hey, c'mon. How hard can it be? Every few hours you put a new diaper on her head. Right?

GLORIA. Christy, please. I don't want to be alone. Please, please, please. Let me go. I'll be fine.

(Beat.)

CHRISTY. We'll send John.

GLORIA. *John?!* Does he know *anything* about babies? Has he ever *seen* one?

CHRISTY. I don't know. But John can do anything.

GLORIA. What about Maud? We could send her.

CHRISTY. Oh, sure.

GLORIA. Why not?

CHRISTY. Maud? Dealing with all the...lawyers and the paperwork and the immigration? They'd end up in Tibet.

GLORIA. I'll bet she could do it.

CHRISTY. Never.

GLORIA. She could! Honestly!

CHRISTY. No! *(Pause.)* ...I suppose we could send them together.

GLORIA. John and Maud? To San Francisco?

CHRISTY. Yeah.

(Beat. Christy laughs wickedly.)

Oh I'd love to see that. They'd kill each other. The problem is, they wouldn't do it.

GLORIA. Of course they would. For us?! They have to! We need them!

CHRISTY. John'll refuse.

GLORIA. No he won't!

CHRISTY. Gloria, I know him!

GLORIA. At least *talk* to him. All right, please? That can't hurt. And I'll talk to Maud. But it has to be *now,* Christy, before it's too late!

(JOHN and MAUD ENTER from opposite sides.)

> JOHN. *No!*
> MAUD. *No!*
> JOHN. *Absolutely not!*
> MAUD. *You must be out of your mind!*
> CHRISTY. John!
> GLORIA. Maud!
> CHRISTY. Please.
> GLORIA. Please, please!
> CHRISTY. John.
> JOHN & MAUD. *NO!!!*

(Blackout. In the darkness we hear:)

ANNOUNCER (PA SYSTEM.) Caledonia Airlines Flight 936 to New York City with connecting flights to Chicago, Denver and San Francisco is now boarding at Gate 14.

(The lights come up on the inside of the airport as JOHN and MAUD head for the gate. CHRISTY is with them just to help.)

MAUD. *(Fussing)* I've got my wallet…my passport…Do you have your passport?

JOHN. Yes –

MAUD. And the address?

JOHN. Yes, yes! We've been over this a thousand times! All right?! I've got everything! I'll be right back. I need to use the gents.

MAUD. It's called the "bathroom" in America. Don't

forget, the expressions are different over there. *(JOHN walks away with a frustrated sigh. MAUD continues her explanation to CHRISTY.)* In America, you don't "ring" someone up, you call them up. You don't "knock someone up." You knock on the door.

MAUD. To knock someone up means, well...you know...to have...relations.

CHRISTY. Sorry, what?

MAUD. I said to "knock someone up" means something different in America.

CHRISTY. I can't hear you!

ANNOUNCER (PA SYSTEM). This is your final call for Caledonia Airlines Flight 936 to New York City, with connecting flights to Chicago, Denver and San Francisco.

Please proceed to Gate 14.

Final call for Caledonia Airlines Flight 936.

(The announcer stops abruptly.)

MAUD. IT MEANS HAVING SEXUAL INTERCOURSE!!

(She looks around, mortified that she's just been heard by everyone in the terminal. JOHN RETURNS.)

JOHN. All right, let's go. They said final call. Take care, my lad.

MAUD. Christy, please take care of Gloria, she means everything to me.

CHRISTY. I will, I promise.

MAUD. She's a delicate girl, like her mother.

CHRISTY. I know –
MAUD. But I know she'll make you a good wife always.
CHRISTY. Of course she will.
MAUD. Like her mother —
JOHN. *Would you come on, woman, and stop the palaver!*
MAUD. *All right, all right! (JOHN stalks off.)* Good-bye,
Christy. Tell Gloria I love her!

*(MAUD hurries off leaving CHRISTY alone. The lights fade
quickly, then come up on the first class section of Caledonia Airlines, Flight 936.)*

STEWARDESS. *(Over PA system.)* Please take your seats,
ladies and gentlemen. We apologize for the short delay, but the
doors are now closing and the plane will be pulling out from the
gate momentarily.

*(JOHN and MAUD ENTER at the top of the aisle. MAUD is
looking around at everything on the plane, which is obviously unfamiliar to her. She's very spooked, but is trying
to act calm. JOHN is grumpy and annoyed, but trying to
be tolerant.)*

MAUD. ...It's very small in here. I had no idea. Planes
look so much bigger from the outside. I suppose it's an optical
illusion of some kind...

(They reach their row.)
JOHN. Aisle or window?
MAUD. Sorry?

JOHN. Aisle or window. Which seat would you prefer?

MAUD. ... I have no idea.

JOHN. Take the window. You'll see more. And you could jump out of it.

MAUD. It's very stuffy in here. Is it always this stuffy?

(A VERY FAT PASSENGER squeezes by them.)

PASSENGER. Sorry, sorry.

JOHN. Sorry.

MAUD. Sorry.

PASSENGER. Sorry.

(He's gone.)

MAUD. All these people.

JOHN. You should see it back there.

MAUD. Where?

JOHN. Back there! Behind the curtain. In the regular class.

MAUD. There are *more* people? Are you sure? *(JOHN sighs in disbelief. MAUD walks up the aisle and peeks behind the curtain.)* Oh my God, it's like Calcutta!

(The STEWARDESS comes by.)

STEWARDESS. *(To MAUD.)* Could you find your seat, please. We'll be taking off in a moment.

MAUD. ... Sorry?

JOHN. Over here! She wants you to sit down!

MAUD. Oh. Sorry. *(She squeezes by the Passenger we saw*

before, who's now going back the other way.) Sorry.
      PASSENGER. Sorry.
      MAUD. So sorry.

*(MAUD takes her seat, and JOHN sits beside her, on the aisle.
She looks extremely anxious. We hear the crackle of the
plane's PA system, and the CAPTAIN makes an announcement.)*

      CAPTAIN. This is your Captain speaking. Please fasten
your seat belts, and keep them fastened until further notice. We
should be airborne presently. Thank you.

*(This being a plane, not a word of the announcement was intel-
ligible to the human ear.)*

      MAUD. What did he say?
      JOHN. I have no idea.

*(MAUD can't find her seat belt, so JOHN tries to help her. He
has trouble finding one of the ends, and reaches around
her so that his hand is under MAUD'S rear end. At this
moment, the PASSENGER passes.)*

      PASSENGER. *(Reacting to JOHN seemingly groping
MAUD.)* Sorry.
      JOHN. Sorry.

      (JOHN finally gets her buckled in.)
      MAUD. What if someone died during the flight. What
would they do with him?

JOHN. I suppose they'd pop him out one of the windows.

(The plane lurches as it begins to move.)

MAUD. *AAAAAAHH!*
JOHN. *Shh!*
MAUD. *What happened?!*
JOHN. The plane is moving. It's supposed to move.
MAUD. Oh. I see...It moved. ...It's supposed to...

(MAUD takes a deep breath and tries to calm herself. We now realize that MAUD is that hysterically nervous flyer who is buried deeply in all of us. The sounds and movements of the plane set off a phobic, hysterical reaction.)

MAUD. ... I think I should tell you something. I *AHHH!*... I've never flown before. In a plane. *(She laughs nervously.)* In a plane. I suppose that's the only way to fly, isn't it.
JOHN. *(Giving her a look.)* Not necessarily.

(The plane lurches again.)

MAUD. *AAAAAHH! AHH! AHH! AHH!*

(She grabs JOHN'S arm in real desperation.)

JOHN. What are you doing?!
MAUD. I'm sorry, I'm sorry. It's just. It's just. It's not supposed to do *that*, is it?! That-that-that *lurch*. I mean a *second* time ...
JOHN. Of course it is. It's just startin' and stoppin' like a bloody car.

(The plane lurches forward again.)

MAUD. *AHHHHHH!!!*

(JOHN rolls his eyes, and the STEWARDESS APPEARS.)

STEWARDESS. Madam, are you all right?
MAUD. I'm fine, I'm fine, I'm fine...
STEWARDESS. Can I get you something? A pillow?
MAUD. *(To the STEWARDESS.)* The plane is moving. It's supposed to move.
JOHN. Bring her a Rob Roy.

(The STEWARDESS EXITS.)

MAUD. *(Agitated)* I never should have agreed to this. I said we should take a ship. A ship is *civilized.* It may take a few more days, but it's *safe. (Lurch) AHH!*
JOHN. There is nothin' to be frightened of.
MAUD. *(Babbling)* I took a ship once, to the Greek islands. It was delightful. They-they had entertainment. And-and-and deck chairs. Beautiful deck chairs. With canvas on them.
STEWARDESS. *(Reappearing with a glass and handing it to MAUD.)* Here we are. I'll come back when we're aloft.

(She EXITS.)

MAUD. *(Closing her eyes.)* Corfu. I'll think about Corfu.
JOHN. Have a drink while you're at it.

(The noise of the plane's engines suddenly increases, and the plane starts to shake as it takes off. MAUD opens her eyes.)

MAUD. ... What's rattling? Why is everything rattling?! All at once?! *The plane is coming apart! IT'S COMING APART!*
JOHN. Take a drink before it spills!

(MAUD takes a drink...and immediately starts coughing and sputtering and gasping for air.)

MAUD. Oh God! Oh my God! What *is* it?! Ohh! Ohh! *AHH! AHH!*

(She keeps coughing and screaming. She can't get her breath. JOHN slaps her on her back. After a great deal of commotion, she settles down, though she's still panting and holding her throat. As she pants, she realizes that the noise and rattling have stopped and have been replaced by a comforting hum. She looks around, then sighs deeply.)

MAUD. Oh, thank God. Listen. There's a gentle hum. Do you hear it? Let's get off before they try *that* again.
JOHN. We can't. We're in the air.
MAUD. Sorry?
JOHN. We're *flying*. We're in the *air.*

(MAUD looks at him as though he's lost his mind. Then she looks out the window...and without thinking, she picks up the glass and drinks the rest. Immediately, she starts

coughing and gasping again. JOHN shakes his head. The lights fade. We hear in the darkness:)

CAPTAIN. *(Over PA system.)* Ladies and gentlemen, this is your captain speaking. We have now reached our cruising altitude of 35,000 feet. Our flying time to New York City is approximately seven hours and fifteen minutes. Please keep your seatbelts fastened when you're in your seats, as we're likely to hit quite a bit of turbulence this trip.

(The lights come up. It's two hours later. MAUD is slumped in her seat, snoring loudly. There are three empty glasses in front of her. The plane is bumping quite a bit, but she's oblivious to it. JOHN glances at her, to make sure she's asleep. Then he goes back to reading his copy of "Doctor Spock on Baby Care.")
As the lights fade, we hear Elvis Presley singing "You Ain't Nothin' But A Hound Dog." The lights come up on the living room of a hotel suite in San Francisco. Elvis's song is coming out of a radio on one of the tables. After a moment, we hear a knock on the door to the hall. No answer. Then more knocking. MAUD ENTERS from one of the two bedrooms off the living room. She looks pretty much worse for wear, and her head is killing her. She's buttoning the sleeves of her blouse, just getting dressed for the day. As she passes the radio, she looks at it quizzically, turns it off and opens the door. DIMITRI, a waiter, ENTERS, a friendly fellow carrying a tray. He has an Eastern European accent.)
DIMITRI. You order breakfast?
MAUD. Yes, come in. Could you put it here?

DIMITRI. Sure. Why not. You should open curtain. Is beautiful day out. Okay?

MAUD. All right. *(The WAITER opens the curtains and sunlight floods into the room, adding to MAUD'S headache.)* I'm afraid I overslept. In fact, I seem to have lost an entire day somewhere.

DIMITRI. Is no big deal. I lose days all the time. After my brother's wedding, I lose whole week. *(He lifts the tray cover.)* Eggs ham bacon oatmeal you don't say what so I bring everything. Coffee toast danish is very fresh. You need more, you holler. Ask for Ivan.

MAUD. Is your name Ivan?

DIMITRI. No, I'm Dimitri.

MAUD. Thank you. Oh. Wait. *(She goes to her purse and gives him a tip.)* This is for you.

DIMITRI. *(Looks at the tip sadly.)* Okay....Oh. I almost forget. Your husband say to tell you he will be back soon. Is doing errands.

MAUD. My "husband?"

DIMITRI. Yah.

MAUD. What do you mean my *"husband"?*

DIMITRI. Husband. Tickle tickle in bed.

MAUD. I know what a husband is!

DIMITRI. Mr. Camp Bell.

MAUD. "Campbell." And he is *not* my husband!

DIMITRI. Oh. You are kept woman.

MAUD. No. I am not a "kept woman." Did Mr. Campbell *say* he was my husband?

DIMITRI. Uh, no. But same room...

MAUD. There are *two bedrooms* in this suite, young man. Which is why we chose this particular hotel.

DIMITRI. Is nice hotel. Romantic. Good for tickle tickle...

MAUD. We are here on business!. Please tell the staff. And the management. And anyone else you can think of!

DIMITRI. Okay. Sorry. I go.

(As he goes for the door, JOHN ENTERS carrying an armful of purchases. He seems unusually chipper.)

JOHN. *(To the WAITER.)* Hello Dimitri! Nice to see you again!

DIMITRI. Breakfast over there. Next to your wife. Good luck.

(DMITRI EXITS and closes the door.)

MAUD. Did you hear that?! Hm?! That man? He thinks we're married! And so, apparently, does everyone else in this hotel!

(Beat. JOHN bursts into a hearty laugh. Then:)

JOHN. You're joking.

MAUD. No.

JOHN. I hope you set him straight.

MAUD. Of course I did.

JOHN. *(Putting down his packages.)* They're a strange lot, these Americans. But I like 'em. They've got real heart. And this city, it's wonderful! It's built on hills, you know. Quite invigoratin'. And wait'll you see the bridge! It's called the Golden Gate.

MAUD. You're in a good mood.

JOHN. I feel very...free in this country. Very much my own self. And I like the people. They all talk like John Wayne. *(Imitating John Wayne.)* "The hotel is two blocks thataway, pilgrim..." So. Here it is. What do you think?

(He has pulled out a grocery carrier with a handle and is displaying it proudly.)

MAUD. What is it?

JOHN. To carry the baby! I got it from a grocery store. So what do you think it cost us? Guess. ...Three dollars.

MAUD. That's not a bassinet.

JOHN. Well o' course not. A real bassinet is upwards o' twenty dollars. It's highway robbery! And this does exactly the same thing. Three dollars.

MAUD. I don't believe it.

JOHN. Nor did I. But it's the gospel. I also got everything else on the list. Look at this. Nightshirt. *(He pulls out a child's nightshirt big enough for a three-year-old.)* With *duckies* on it.

MAUD. Don't you think it's a bit big?

JOHN. I thought o' that. So I got her a belt, just in case. *(He pulls out the belt.)* Bottle. Nipple for bottle.

MAUD. You got *one* bottle?

JOHN. And one nipple. One is plenty. You wash 'em after every meal. *(He pulls out more surprises.)* Nappie. They call it a diaper.

MAUD. You didn't buy just *one?*

JOHN. *(Scornfully)* Of course not. Here's the other one. And here's the pin. It was over-priced, but I had no choice.

MAUD. *(Coldly)* Is that everything?

JOHN. No. I saved the best for last. The crowning glory. *(He pulls out a pair of Mickey Mouse Club ears.)* Mouse ears. Mickey Mouse. He's very popular over here. They've got a club or somethin'. She can wear 'em on her head. She'll love it.

MAUD. Give me the list.

JOHN. Why?

MAUD. Give me the list! I obviously have some shopping to do.

JOHN. I did the shopping!

MAUD. There is no child on earth who has only two nappies. You need at least a dozen.

JOHN. *A dozen*?!

MAUD. And where's the blanket?

JOHN. There's two on my bed. She can have one o' those. And she can have my pillow too.

MAUD. Give me the list! Now!

JOHN. *(Handing it over.)* Fine! Do what you want!

MAUD. *(Getting her purse.)* I'll be back by lunch time.

JOHN. Don't do me any favors. You can take your time! *(She heads for the door.)* And be it on your head if the child is spoiled! *(She EXITS, slamming the door. To himself:)* You are easily the most impossible woman that ever lived. *(He starts putting his purchases back in the bags.)* It's no wonder you never married. You'd drive a sane man to the bug house...*(The phone rings, and he answers it.)* Hello? ...Yes it is.... Ah, Miss Merchant. We've been expectin' your call.... We are indeed. And we're anxious to meet the little tyke....*(He goes white.)* What? ...You're jokin'. ...You're downstairs with the baby now?...Come up? Uh, sure. That-that-that's grand.... Yes, I'm right here. I'll be waitin'. *(He hangs up in a dazed panic ... then runs out of the room, and we hear him calling for MAUD off-stage:)* Miss Kinch!...*Miss Kinch*!!...*(He hurries back into the room, to the telephone, and dials.)*

      JOHN. *(Cont'd)* Hello, front desk? It's Mr. Campbell, room 806. Miss Kinch should be comin' out o' the lift any second and I want you to stop her....Maud Kinch.... About fifty. Hair like straw. A very dowdy person. No, she's not my wife! *(Horrified:)* ...She did?! She left already?! Are ya sur... Well what the hell good are you?!! *(He hangs up; and immediately there's a knock on the door.)* Holy Christ.

(He doesn't know what to do, but finally opens the door. BEV-ERLY MERCHANT ENTERS, a friendly woman holding an infant in her arms. The infant is wrapped in a blanket. JOHN looks stunned.)

      JOHN. Come in, come in...
      BEVERLY. Here she is.

(JOHN looks at the baby for the first time, and he's awestruck. Mesmerized. From this point on, JOHN is in another world.)

      BEVERLY. Would you like to hold her?
      JOHN. ... I would. Yes. *(She hands the baby to JOHN. He can't take his eyes off her.)* ...She's a little thing.
      BEVERLY. She's two weeks old.
      JOHN. Two weeks old...
      BEVERLY. I'm sorry I'm early, but I have two more placements today. I hope it's all right. *(No response.)* Mr. Campbell ...?

JOHN. Hm?

BEVERLY. I said I'm sorry I'm early.

JOHN. It's fine...

BEVERLY. Is Miss Kinch here?

JOHN. *(To the baby.)* What a pretty little girl you are.... She's got my finger.

BEVERLY. She's a real heartbreaker. She hardly cries at all. She has a great disposition.

JOHN. Hello...

BEVERLY. I'll need to see some identification, and you'll have to sign a release. We'll do the real paperwork next Friday, before we go to court. It is on Friday, by the way. The judge had to postpone for a few days. He had some minor surgery.

(JOHN hasn't heard a word of this. He's completely wrapped up in the baby.)

JOHN. She's very sweet. Look at her...*(Then:)* Uh oh. I think she's wet. Or somethin' else maybe. *(Sniff)*

BEVERLY. Do you want to change her?

JOHN. Not in this lifetime.

BEVERLY. Sure you do. Put her down. We'll do it together. Have you ever changed a baby?

JOHN. Un-uhn..

BEVERLY. Unpin her. I'll get some water. *(She heads for the bathroom and EXITS, calling:)* Do you have a clean diaper?

JOHN. *(Calling back.)* Is one diaper enough?!

BEVERLY. Sure!

JOHN. I knew it, I knew it!

(The lights fade quickly. They come back up on JOHN, sitting in a chair in the living room, holding the baby in his lap, giving her a bottle. There's no one else in the room. Elvis Presley's recording of "Heartbreak Hotel" is playing quietly on the radio.)

JOHN. Ach. Just look at you. What a good little baby you are. You've got such pretty blue eyes. And those lashes! There are girls all over Scotland'd give big money for lashes like those. You must use...what do you call that stuff?...Maybelline. *(A gurgle.)* Aha. Your Uncle John made you smile with that one, eh? Ooh, I like that grin. It's all gums. Whup. Back to the bottle. Sorry. You must have missed breakfast the way you're goin' at it. *(Pause; he watches her.)* Shlurp, shlurp, shlurp. *(Same)* Aren't you the beauty o' the world. *(Same)* Uh oh. Not much left. A-a-a-a-and gone. Every drop. Good girl. Shall we try a burp, huh? Now let's see, how do we do this... *(He spreads a cloth on his shoulder and hoists the baby up.)* There. Not so hard when you know what you're doin'. *(He pats her back.)* How's that? Do you feel all right? *(Pat pat pat — then the baby gives a loud burp.)* Whoa! That was a good one! You almost blew me out the window. They must have heard that back in Aberdeen.

(We hear a key in the lock, then MAUD ENTERS, carrying her purchases.)

MAUD. Well, I'm glad that's out of the way. I found a department store, and an excellent chemist, they call it a "pharmacy" over here, and they had everything I...*(And then she sees that JOHN is holding the baby.)* ...What's that?

JOHN. *(Proudly)* What do you think it is.

MAUD. ...She's here? How did she -? ....Oh my God, she's gorgeous! Look at her! She's stunning! Oh, my dear child. How on earth —?

JOHN. The lass from the agency brought her early. She had a busy day or somethin'.

MAUD. They just ..dropped her off? With you?

JOHN. About two hours ago. Just after you left.

MAUD. Are they out of their minds?! You don't know anything about babies! *(Trying to take the baby from JOHN.)* Oh, you poor sweetheart! Come to Auntie Maud. I'll take care of you.

JOHN. I've got her just fine.

MAUD. You poor little thing.

JOHN. She's not a "poor little thing." She's happy as a lark.

MAUD. *Careful! Support her head! You have to support her head!*

JOHN. *I'm supportin' her head!*

("WHAAAAAA!" The baby starts to cry and continues to cry throughout the following. MAUD takes her out of JOHN'S arms.)

MAUD. You poor thing. You'll be fine. Auntie Maud is here...

JOHN. *(Getting increasingly angry.)* Now look what you've done.

MAUD. You'll be all right...

JOHN. She was all right before you walked in that door!

THE BABY. *WHAAAAAAAAAAAAAA!!!!*

MAUD. Are you hungry? Maybe she's hungry.

JOHN. I just fed her!

MAUD. Well something's the matter!

JOHN. You were shoutin' in her face, that's what the matter is!

MAUD. Her head was lolling backwards! You can't do that! *("WHAAAAAA!")* You're fine now, sweetheart. Don't cry. *("WHAAAAAA!")* You're going to be a-a-a-all right...

JOHN. *(Blood in his eye.)* Give her to me.

MAUD. Don't be ridiculous.

JOHN. I want her back.

MAUD. I'm holding her now, thank you very much.

JOHN. *(Almost brutally angry.) Give her back to me this instant!*

(MAUD is startled. Silence. Even the baby has stopped crying. Then the baby starts to cry again...and MAUD, without a word, hands her over to JOHN.)

JOHN. *(Quietly)* Shhh...It's all right, sweetie. Everything's okay...

(MAUD watches him for a moment, her face as white as a sheet. She's ready to cry. But instead she straightens up and walks out of the room, closing the door behind her.)

JOHN. ...Shhh...There's nothin' to be afraid of....Shhh ... That's my girl.

(The lights fade. They come back up on MAUD, sitting alone in the living room with a book on her lap, staring sadly into

*the distance. Then JOHN ENTERS from his bedroom. She
stiffens. She doesn't look at him. He looks around the room,
finds his watch on a table and straps it on. Not a word is
spoken. MAUD pretends to read. Finally:)*

MAUD. Where's the baby?
JOHN. She's on a cruise ship to the Aegean.
MAUD. I meant what is she doing.
JOHN. She's asleep. And it's about time.
MAUD. Good.
JOHN. I have to go see that lawyer fella. The court date is
postponed till Friday. Beverly told me.
MAUD. I see. So *I* have to stay with *you,* here in San Fran-
cisco for an extra *five days.* Is that it? Is that what you're say-
ing?
JOHN. *(Angrily)* That's exactly what I'm sayin', and I'm
sorry for the inconvenience!

*(He stomps out, slamming the door...which wakes the baby.
"WHAAAAA!" MAUD hurries into the bedroom and comes
out, carrying the baby.)*

MAUD. You're all right. You'll be just fine. That nasty
man just slammed the door and woke you up. *(The telephone
rings.)* Oh, dear...Oh...*(Her hands are full. Ring! She juggles
the baby and manages to get the phone.)* Hello? ...Yes it is....
So you're Beverly. How do you do. I'm sorry I missed you, I
had no idea...Yes, she is beautiful. I'm holding her right now.
...Yes, I do know about Friday, but if you could possibly do it
sooner, you see, this man I'm here with isn't exactly the person
that I would choose to...Oh. Ah. I see. Well it's Friday, then.

Hm? …Yes, he does do well with the baby. I was quite surprised also. Good-bye.

(As she hangs up, JOHN REENTERS. They look at each other warily, squaring off. MAUD is holding the baby.)

JOHN. I forgot something. …Is that her?

MAUD. No, it's Cleopatra.

JOHN. Did you wake her up?

MAUD. Of course not! *You* woke her when you slammed the door. Poor thing…Incidentally, the agency just rang. Beverly. Just checking up. She was quite impressed with the way you handled the baby.

JOHN. She seems a good lass.

MAUD. I'm sure you think so.

(JOHN angrily goes out the front door of the suite and leaves. In the hall, he changes his mind and comes back into the room. MAUD gets very interested in tending the baby, ignoring JOHN entirely.)

JOHN. Look…*(He wants to say something, but instead, he pulls out a gift-wrapped package and hands it to MAUD.)* Here. It's for you.

MAUD. For me?

JOHN. It is your birthday, I believe.

MAUD. Gloria told you.

JOHN. And Christy. *(MAUD looks at the present. She doesn't know what to say.)* Are you going to open it or not?

(She unwraps the present. It's a book. She opens it to the title page.)

MAUD. Robert Burns.

JOHN. My favorite. I believe he's from Scotland.

MAUD. ... Thank you. I'm sure I'll enjoy it.

(Silence. JOHN reluctantly heads for his bedroom. Then:)

MAUD & JOHN. *(Simultaneously)* Mr. Campbell — Miss Kinch —

JOHN. Go ahead.

MAUD. *(With difficulty.)* I'm sorry about just now. I shouldn't have snatched the baby that way. I frequently do things that I later regret.

JOHN. I shouldn't have shouted the way I did. It was un-called for. I'm sorry.

MAUD. Thank you.

JOHN. We'll have to share a bit.

MAUD. Yes, I know. Also, I think we should try not to argue in front of her. She's been through enough already.

JOHN. I agree entirely. She comes first.

MAUD. Agreed.

(Pause.)

MAUD. Would you like to hold her?

JOHN. I would.

(They transfer the baby.)

MAUD. Be careful...

JOHN. *(Holding her.)*

Ach. What a beauty.

"She is a winsome wee thing,
She is a handsome wee thing,
She is a lonesome wee thing,
This wee, sweet child o' mine."

(The lights fade. In the darkness, we hear a telephone ring. The lights come up on CHRISTY answering the call and JOHN placing it.)

CHRISTY. Hello?

JOHN. Christy?

CHRISTY. John! What's the matter?!

JOHN. There's nothin' the matter. We're all doin' fine.

CHRISTY. How's the baby?

JOHN. She's gettin' cuter by the minute. They'll have to put her on Ed Sullivan next.

CHRISTY. On what?

JOHN. "Ed Sullivan." On the telly. He has singers and things.

CHRISTY. Why would you put her on the telly?

JOHN. No, ya clod!

CHRISTY. She's only three weeks old.

JOHN. It was a joke! I mean she's special! She's unusual. Like...Elvis Presley or somethin'.

CHRISTY. ...She looks like Elvis Presley?

JOHN. *Just forget it!* Forget I said anything! Christ!... Now listen, lad, they've had to postpone the hearing for a second time. The judge is still recoverin' from an operation or somethin'.

CHRISTY. Oh, no.

JOHN. It can't be helped. They've got it scheduled now for

a week Monday.

CHRISTY. Can't they get another judge?

JOHN. I tried that. They won't do it. Now look, have you picked a name yet?

CHRISTY. No.

JOHN. Christ!

CHRISTY. We're trying! We just...can't agree. On anything lately.

JOHN. Well try harder! They want a name when we get to court.

CHRISTY. Look, if you don't hear from us in time, just... pick something. We can change it when she gets here.

JOHN. You don't want to confuse the poor little thing.

(GLORIA ENTERS, carrying her coat.)

GLORIA. Who is it?

CHRISTY. It's John. They're fine. The court date is postponed again.

GLORIA. Oh ...balls! Can't they do anything?!

CHRISTY. No.

GLORIA. It's not fair.

CHRISTY. And they need a name for the baby.

GLORIA. I told you her name.

CHRISTY. I am not naming my daughter "Herpatia." Where did you get that?!

GLORIA. It was my grandmother's name. She died when she was thirty.

CHRISTY. Probably from embarrassment.

GLORIA. Oh, grow up.

(She starts to EXIT.)

CHRISTY. Wait. Where are you going?

GLORIA. I told you this morning! I'm going shopping in Aberdeen. The great metropolis. You know, the one that hasn't any fashions or cafes or theatres.

CHRISTY. Oh. Right *(She EXITS. Calling:)* Have fun!

JOHN. Are you still there?!

CHRISTY. Yeah. So how's everything else? How's Maud?

JOHN. She's a pain in the arse, but she'd say exactly the same about me, so there you go. Look, we're wastin' money here. Call us when you have the name.

CHRISTY. John? What do you think of... "Herpatia"?

JOHN. Her what?

CHRISTY. *Herpatia.* As a name for the baby.

JOHN. I think you need your head examined.

CHRISTY. *(Glum)* Yeah, I know.

JOHN. What's her nickname goin' to be? "Herpes?"

CHRISTY. I *know.*

JOHN. I suppose her middle name could be "Syndrome."

CHRISTY. It's not *my* idea.

(MAUD ENTERS.)

MAUD. John, I can't find the nappies. Where did you put them?

JOHN. In the bottom drawer.

MAUD. I tried that. They're not there.

JOHN. Okay, I'm comin', Maud me girl. Christy. Work on the name and stop horsin' around. Ya get it?! G'bye.

(JOHN hangs up, and his light fades. CHRISTY starts to hang

up, then looks at the phone.)

CHRISTY. "Maud me girl"...?

As CHRISTY hangs up, we hear the murmur of voices and the clinking of china, and we cross fade to a restaurant in San Francisco. The MAITRE D', who thinks quite well of himself, and the WAITRESS, who doesn't, speak as they help change the scene.)

WAITRESS. Do we really have room for another table?
MAITRE D'. My dear, it's called the restaurant business. It involves the exchange of currency.
WAITRESS. But it's so near the kitchen.
MAITRE D'. And just think how hot the food will be.

(JOHN and MAUD ENTER the restaurant, pushing the baby carriage.)

MAITRE D'. May I help you?
JOHN. We have a reservation in the name of Mr. Campbell.
MAITRE D'. Right this way, please....Will this be all right?
MAUD. That's lovely, thank you.

(They sit, the baby carriage closest to MAUD.)

MAITRE D'. We're completely full-up, of course, but I have managed to find you one of our best tables. And this is a little complimentary sorbet to cleanse the palate. I hope you enjoy it.

(He holds his hand out for a tip – and JOHN shakes it.)

JOHN. *(Proudly, to the MAITRE D', nodding across the table.)* Thanks. It's her first time in a restaurant.
MAITRE D'. *(Thinking he means MAUD.)...Really?*
JOHN. I hope she behaves herself.
MAITRE D'. *(Glancing at MAUD.)* So do I. *(To MAUD, as though addressing an idiot.)* This-is-the-menu. I-hope-you-enjoy-it.

(He hands menus to MAUD and JOHN, then EXITS. JOHN and MAUD look at each other – and they burst into laughter.)

MAUD. Thank you very much. Now he thinks I'm an imbecile....Is it warm in here? I think she's too warm.
JOHN. I think she could do without the blanket.
MAUD. I think you're right.

(MAUD removes the blanket.)

JOHN. Look at that smile.
MAUD. She likes going out. She likes people.
JOHN. That's a very flatterin' dress she's wearin'. Good choice.
MAUD. You picked it.
JOHN. Yes, I know. There's a picture o' me somewhere, about six months old, wearin' very much the same outfit. I look adorable.
MAUD. I'll believe that when I see it.

(They open their menus. Beat. Then JOHN reacts:)

JOHN. Christ! Would you look at these prices! If they charged any more money, they'd be arrested for larceny.

MAUD. It's not so bad.

JOHN. "Not so bad"?! Have you lost your eyesight?!

MAUD. I'll tell you what. We can order one dinner. And you can watch me eat it.

JOHN. Ha, ha. That's a real knee-slapper.

MAUD. Oh, don't be such a...

JOHN. What?

MAUD. Nothing.

JOHN. *What?* You were goin' to say "cheapskate," weren't you.

MAUD. I wouldn't dream of it...You did say it was my birthday dinner.

JOHN. It is, it is. Forget I said a word. Put it out o' your mind.

MAUD. Thank you.

(They go back to their menus. Pause.)

JOHN. I can always take out a loan.

MAUD. Look, why don't we go Dutch Treat. I'll pay for my half. We'll enjoy it more.

JOHN. No, no ...

MAUD. I insist.

JOHN. It's out of the question!...If you want to think about that sort of thing, we should go Scotch Treat.

MAUD. Oh? What's that?

JOHN. You pay for the whole dinner.

MAUD. *(Standing up.)* That's it, I'm leaving.
JOHN. It was a joke! Christ! Would you sit down!

(As MAUD sits, the MAITRE D' and the WAITRESS come to the table.)

MAITRE D'. This is Lorraine. She'll be your server.

(He takes the sorbets back and leaves.)

WAITRESS. Good evening. Can I get you a drink?
MAUD. Yes. I'll have a...oh, what's it called?...a Rob Roy.
JOHN. You're jokin'.
MAUD. No.
JOHN. The last time you had one, you slept for fourteen hours.
MAUD. A Rob Roy, please.
JOHN. I'll have the same. *(Referring to the baby:)* She'll stick to her milk.
MAUD. *(To the WAITRESS.)* She's three weeks old today.
WAITRESS. *(She couldn't be less interested.)* Really?
JOHN. She looks older, but that's because she has such strong features.
MAUD. And such long hair.
JOHN. Her hair's a picture, don't you think?
WAITRESS. Hm? Very nice. I'll be back with your drinks.

(The WAITRESS EXITS. JOHN and MAUD are outraged.)
JOHN. ... "Very nice?" That's all she has to say?!

MAUD. The girl is a complete idiot.

JOHN. Or blind as a bat!

MAUD. Some people.

JOHN. It's unbelievable! You'd have to be a moron not to see she's one in a million. This is not your average child!

MAUD. The girl obviously knows nothing about children. Less than nothing. Minus nothing.

JOHN. She can forget about a tip, I'll tell you that.

(Beat. Then they look into the carriage and smile.)

JOHN. Look at her.

MAUD. She looks especially beautiful tonight. I think it's the bath.

JOHN. Aye.

MAUD. She starts to glow after the bath, as if there's a light inside her.

(The WAITRESS arrives with the drinks, smiling, oblivious to her gaffe. JOHN and MAUD both scowl at her.)

WAITRESS. Here we are. For you, madam. And you, sir.

JOHN. You're a right mess, aren't you.

WAITRESS. I'm sorry?

MAUD. Don't look at me. I agree with him.

(The WAITRESS goes, totally confused.)

JOHN. Well...cheers.

MAUD. Cheers.

JOHN. To your natal day. Seven days late.

MAUD. Thank you.

(MAUD sips her drink carefully and breathes deeply. She's determined to get it right. Pause. They enjoy the moment. Then:)

JOHN. Shall we get down to work?
MAUD. Let's.

(They each pull out a pad and a pencil and flip to the correct page. All very business-like. They could be at a board meeting.)

JOHN. Right.
MAUD. Uh, Genevieve. Gen
JOHN. Too Frenchy. What about Mary?
MAUD. I must know ten Marys, and I don't like any of them.
JOHN. Penelope.
MAUD. Janice.
JOHN. Marigold.
MAUD. Marigold?
JOHN. Sorry. Forget it.
MAUD. Angela.
JOHN. Christina.
MAUD. Jessica.

(The lights shift to a moonlit park. JOHN and MAUD are strolling back to their hotel, still working on names. MAUD is pushing the carriage and JOHN has his notebook out.)
JOHN. Hester.

MAUD. Barbara.

JOHN. Elizabeth.

MAUD. Abigail.

JOHN. Let's try some Shakespeare names. That should do the trick.

MAUD. Juliet.

JOHN. Ophelia.

MAUD. Rosalind.

JOHN. Celia.

MAUD. Jaquenetta.

JOHN. Mustardseed.

MAUD. We're getting silly.

JOHN. Helena.

MAUD. Miranda.

JOHN. ...Ooh, I like *that.* Miranda. The Tempest is one o' my favorite plays.

MAUD. Mine, too. Write it down.

(He does. Then he sits down heavily on a bench, glad for the rest. She joins him.)

JOHN. The more we do this, the more I feel like my old friend Jack Falstaff.

MAUD. You mean you ate too much.

JOHN. No. He says at one point, "I would to God thou and I knew where a commodity of *good names* were to be bought." Henry Four, Part One.

MAUD. Of course. How silly of me.

(She rolls her eyes.)

JOHN. "Jack" is a good name. What about Jacqueline?

We'd call her Jack.

MAUD. *(Stiffening almost imperceptibly.)* No.

JOHN. I like it. I think we're on to somethin'.

MAUD. I said no!

JOHN. Why not?

MAUD. Do I need a reason?

JOHN. No. I guess not.

(Beat.)

MAUD. I knew someone named Jack.

JOHN. And you didn't like him.

MAUD. On the contrary. I liked him a great deal. *(Pause)* He was my husband.

JOHN. ...You're joking.

MAUD. I was eighteen. He was killed in the war. In the trenches at Passchendaele.

JOHN. I'm sorry.

MAUD. When I think about it, I get very, very angry. I think about it too much.

JOHN. I'm very sorry.

(Pause.)

MAUD. Shall I tell you something? ...After it happened, I stopped believing in God. *(Pause)* Up to that time, I'd been a very good Christian. I went to church, I sang in the choir, I said my prayers, I even tried to think about what God was telling us, trying to tell us, about right from wrong. And then it happened. It just ...happened. A telegram. One moment Jack was alive, and then he wasn't. And I thought, how can anyone in the universe be so cruel. *(Pause)* I tried to pray after that, but it never felt the same, it felt like...insurance. So I gave it up.

JOHN. Do you still feel that way?

MAUD. I don't know. When I look at...

JOHN. Mustardseed.

MAUD. When I look at her, I think I can see him again. In her eyes. Deep in the center of her pupils. He's looking out at me.

JOHN. Who? Jack or God?

MAUD. Jack....Both....I don't know. But for the first time in a hundred years, I feel much better.

(The lights fade as JOHN and MAUD EXIT. The lights come up on CHRISTY, in his house in Scotland, trying out his new television set. It's a big box with a tiny screen, makes a lot of static-noise, and the screen is filled with snow. He fiddles with the knobs and manages to get some sound out of it.)

CHRISTY. Gloria! Look at this! It's starting to work. Tel-ly-vision...It's incredible. Gloria! Come quick! I think I can see a man...no, two men...it might be a woman...

ANNOUNCER. *(Very garbled and full of static.)* Welcome back, ladies and gentlemen. This is the British Broadcasting Company, transmitting to you from London, England, and we hope that you have been enjoying our televisional entertainments this evening...

(It fades out because of the poor reception.)

CHRISTY. *(Coaxing the set, possible hitting the top of it.)* Oh, don't do that, come on, come on...*(The set makes a loud noise and goes off.)* Oh, dammit! I can't believe it! It's supposed to work!

(GLORIA ENTERS, dressed to go out.)

GLORIA. Oh you poor thing. That's your new toy, isn't it. But guess what? In three days you'll have something better to play with. She'll be five weeks old and she'll be right here.

CHRISTY. What are you dressed up for?

GLORIA. The play in Aberdeen? I asked you to come and you said no?

CHRISTY. Oh right.

GLORIA. Life? Human beings? Amusement?

CHRISTY. Are you going with Henry?

GLORIA. My *cousin* Henry. Is there someone else to go with that I don't know about?

CHRISTY. You don't think it looks bad, do you? To other people, I mean.

GLORIA. Of course not. We grew up together. We took *baths* together.

CHRISTY. Is that supposed to make me feel better?

GLORIA. Oh, stop it. …Oh God, I'm late. Don't wait up. *(She kisses him and hurries out.)* Try the telly-thing again!

(She's gone. CHRISTY is annoyed. He turns on the television. He gets some response. Snow, but a person's shadow – and then a voice.)

ANNOUNCER. Thank you for joining us. It's seven o'clock and that ends our day of broadcasting on the British Broadcasting Company. Good night.
(A long electronic sound indicates the station is off the air.

CHRISTY sighs and turns it off.
The lights fade – and then come up in the living room of the hotel suite in San Francisco. JOHN is pacing impatiently, fastening his cuff links. The baby is in her stroller, ready for a journey.)

JOHN. *(Calling off, to MAUD'S room.)* Would you hurry up! We're goin' to be late!

MAUD. *(Off)* I'm coming as fast as I can, there's no use shouting about it!

JOHN. *(To the baby.)* Miranda, don't you ever do this to a man. Do you hear me? Men don't like to wait.

(MAUD ENTERS, fixing her scarf.)

MAUD. I'm ready.

JOHN. It's about time.

MAUD. You are easily the most impatient man that has ever lived. Did you call for a taxi?

JOHN. Yes! I told you that! The car is waiting!

MAUD. Well I'm ready! *(Beat)* Wait. I forgot my gloves.

(She hurries back into her bedroom.)

JOHN. Gloves?! You don't need gloves! We're goin' to court, it's not the vicarage tea party!

MAUD. *(Off)* Do you have all the papers?

JOHN. Of course I've got the papers! You've asked me that ten times!...I better check. *(He pulls some documents from an envelope he's been carrying.)* Immigration...state court petition...health certificate...birth certificate...interstate compact approval...*(To the baby:)* If you ever get lost, the whole country is goin' to light up like a neon sign.

(MAUD ENTERS, carrying her gloves.)

MAUD. I'm ready now.

JOHN. I don't believe you.

MAUD. We have over an hour. Stop being grumpy.

JOHN. *(Putting the papers away.)* I read a book once by that American chap, with the moustache. *(Groping for the name.)* The funny one. He had a partner. With an accent.

MAUD. Leopold and Loeb.

JOHN. Groucho Marx. He said in the preface that he wrote the entire book while waitin' for his wife to get dressed.

MAUD. I'm not your wife.

JOHN. Thank the Lord for that.

MAUD. *(At the door, impatiently.)* Are you ready? I'm waiting.

(JOHN shakes his head — and they leave the room, pulling the front door closed behind them. As soon as the door shuts, they both stop cold.)

MAUD. We forgot the baby.

JOHN. Right. *(MAUD tries the handle, but it's locked.)* Use the key!

MAUD. I don't have the key. You have the key.

JOHN. I thought you had it.

MAUD. Why would I have the key?! You always have the key!

JOHN. You had it yesterday!

MAUD. I went out *alone* yesterday!

JOHN. Christ Almighty.

MAUD. It might be in my other purse…You had to rush me, didn't you.

JOHN. You're not blamin' me for this?!

MAUD. Well it's hardly my fault.

JOHN. *Of course it's your fault, you took four hours to get yourself dressed!*

(Beat. And then the baby starts to wail.)

THE BABY. *WHAAAAAAAAAAAAAA!!!!*

JOHN. Oh my God. She's cryin'.

MAUD. …Miranda?

JOHN. *Miranda?!!*

THE BABY. *WHAAAAAAAAAAAAAA!!!!*

JOHN. Why is she cryin'?

MAUD. Calm down. Crying is what babies do.

JOHN. She could have put somethin' in her mouth! She could be chokin' to death!!

MAUD. *If she was choking to death she wouldn't be crying!* If she's crying, it means she's breathing. If she goes silent, *then* we have to worry. *(Calling out:)* Miranda?! It's Auntie Maud, sweetheart! We'll be right in! All right?! Can you hear me?!

THE BABY. *WHAAAAAAAAAAAAAA!!!!*

JOHN. Move aside.

MAUD. Why?

JOHN. Just move!

MAUD. Oh don't be silly.

JOHN. *Move aside! (Calling)* I'm comin', sweetheart!

Hold your horses!
    MAUD. John!
    JOHN. *(As in "Geronimo!")* AHHHHHHH!

(SLAM!! He hits the door with his whole body. It didn't work. The door is still locked, and JOHN is in pain.)

    JOHN. Ahhhh! Ah! Ah! Ah! Ah!
    THE BABY. *WHAAAAAAAAAAAAAA!!!!*
    MAUD. John! Are you all right?!
    JOHN. I'm fine. *I'm fine!* Ahh! Go downstairs and get the key at the front desk. I'll wait here.
    MAUD. Shall I fetch you a doctor?
    JOHN. Just get the key!
    THE BABY. *WHAAAAAAAAAAAAAA!!!!*
    MAUD. *(Calling)* Miranda, dear. I'm getting the key. I'll be right back.

(MAUD hurries out.)

    JOHN. Ohhh, my arm! Oh, oh, oh, oh. I think it's broken. Ohhh! Christ on a bicycle. Leave it to me. The dolt of Aberdeen. Ahhh! Oooh! *(Pause. No sound at all. Not even the baby. Silence. Then:)* Miranda? *(No response.)* Miranda?! *(No response; genuinely frightened:)* Miranda, it's your Uncle John! Are you all right?! *(Nothing)* MIRANDA?!!! *(Nothing)* Oh, hell. *I'm comin' in, sweetheart! Don't be scared! AHHH-HHHHHH!!!! (JOHN hurls himself at the door and – CRASH! The door bursts open, and JOHN staggers into the room, holding his shoulder.)* Ah! Ah! Ah! Ah!
    THE BABY. *WHAAAAAAAAAAAAAA!!!!*

JOHN. *(Relieved to hear her.)* Oh, thank God. I'm here, sweetness. I'm right here. *(He kneels next to the stroller.)* Are you all right? Huh? Of course you are. I'm right here. That's my girl. I'm right...*(He stops suddenly, and his face goes white. His hand goes to his chest, and he looks confused. He's having a heart attack.)* I'm right... I'm ...Oh my God...Oh my God ...

(He straightens up with the pain. At this moment, MAUD hurries in, followed by DIMITRI.)

MAUD. John? John, how in the world did you...*John!*
JOHN. She's all right. She's fine.
MAUD. What's the matter?!
JOHN. I think I'm havin' ...a heart attack. *Ah!*
MAUD. *John! (To DIMITRI.)* Call an ambulance!
DIMITRI. Mr. Camp bell! Mr. Camp bell! Say something!
MAUD. *Call an ambulance!*

(DMITRI rushes out, leaving MAUD holding JOHN'S head.)

MAUD. Oh, John ...
THE BABY. *WHAAAAAAAAAAAAA!!!!*

(Blackout.)

END OF ACT ONE

ACT II

(We hear music playing: Elvis singing "Let Me Be Your Teddy Bear." The lights come up on JOHN'S hospital room. JOHN is in bed, extremely depressed. His DOCTOR is standing next to him, holding a chart.)

DOCTOR. So we'll continue to monitor your heart, of course, and your vital signs, and I'll want to do some more tests. With any luck, you'll be out on Friday.

JOHN. How about Thursday?

DOCTOR. *(Kindly)* You don't get a door prize for leaving early. I'll be in to see you again tomorrow.

JOHN. Right.

DOCTOR. It's not a bad prognosis.

JOHN. I hear what you're sayin'.

DOCTOR. It's normal to be depressed after a heart attack. You'll feel better soon, I guarantee it.

JOHN. My father died of a heart attack. I'm older than he was.

DOCTOR. We have better medications now. We know more about diet and exercise. And attitude. It's very important.

JOHN. Right. Okay. Thanks.

DOCTOR. I'll see you tomorrow.

(The DOCTOR EXITS. JOHN is alone now. He holds his fore-

head in despair. The NURSE bustles in. She's cheerful and self-important, the kind of well-meaning rattle-brain who never listens to what you're saying. During the following, she goes about her chores with great efficiency.)

NURSE. Good morning! And how are you feeling this fine morning?

JOHN. Tired and depressed, thank you.

NURSE. Oh, now, we don't need the grumps today, do we. Shall I make your bed? Would that be more comfy?

JOHN. No. Thank you.

NURSE. *(Making the bed around him anyway.)* It can be so uncomfortable to sleep in an unmade bed. They get so rumply. But just plump it up and smooth it out and you'll sleep forever.

JOHN. That's what I'm afraid of.

NURSE. *(Checking the plastic pitcher on his bedside table.)* And how's your water today?

JOHN. I'd rather not say.

NURSE. *(Taking the pitcher into the bathroom to fill it up.)* I'll get you a refill.

JOHN. What I'd really like is a nap, if you don't mind. Perhaps you could wake me before lunch time. Could you do that?

NURSE. *(Returning)* What?

JOHN. I said I'd like you to knock me up before lunch.

NURSE. *(Aghast)* ....What did you say?

JOHN. Knock me up. Before lunch. If you don't mind.

NURSE. How dare you.

JOHN. Well I know you're busy, but it shouldn't take you more than a few seconds. *(She gapes at him.)* With all respect, they are payin' you to make me feel better.

NURSE. Mr. Campbell!

JOHN. You don't have to sing me the national anthem while you're doin' it. All I want is a quick bang and a scream.

NURSE. *(Quivering with rage.)* I'm telling your doctor about this. Right now.

(A knock on the door. Then MAUD ENTERS.)

MAUD. May I come in? *(To the NURSE.)* How is he feeling?

NURSE. I would watch him very closely if I were you. Good-bye.

(The NURSE EXITS in a huff.)

MAUD. What's the matter with her?

JOHN. She's got a screw loose or somethin'.

(He yawns, a huge yawn, and lies back on the pillow.)

MAUD. Do you need a nap, or is it just my company?

JOHN. It's the damn pills they shove into me. How's Miranda? Where is she?

MAUD. She's outside entertaining the nurses. How are you feeling?

JOHN. Rotten, if you want the truth.

MAUD. The doctor says you're doing very nicely.

JOHN. The doctor is a big liar. Did you call Christy?

MAUD. I tried but I couldn't get a line through.

JOHN. *(Accusingly)* Why not?

MAUD. I don't know why not. I don't work for the telephone company.

JOHN. You should send him a telegram.

MAUD. I did.

JOHN. ... Oh. Good. Now listen. I've been thinkin' about what has to be done. I made a list. *(He takes a list from his bedside table and consults it.)* First of all, we missed the court date.

MAUD. I'm well aware of that.

JOHN. See if you can make it tomorrow.

MAUD. Don't be silly. I postponed it for another two weeks.

JOHN. What?!

MAUD. I postponed it for two weeks.

JOHN. Why?!

MAUD. I thought you'd want to be there.

JOHN. But if you get the order tomorrow, woman, you can leave on Thursday.

MAUD. Don't be silly. I'm not leaving you here.

JOHN. Why not?

MAUD. Because you're not staying here alone.

JOHN. Of course I can stay here alone.

MAUD. Let's not discuss it. Next.

JOHN. Would you listen to me!

MAUD. Don't get excited. It's not good for you.

JOHN. Holy mother of God.

MAUD. And you can pray after I leave the room.

(He sighs with exasperation.)

JOHN. It's totally ridiculous, you know.

MAUD. Well, I'm just a ridiculous person, aren't I. Go on.

What else?

JOHN. Get a pencil.

MAUD. I'll take your list with me.

JOHN. I want my list!

MAUD. Just read it!

(A stand-off. JOHN sighs again and consults the list.)

JOHN. Number two. Tell the hotel to extend the reservation. For one day.

MAUD. For two weeks. I did that.

JOHN. Three. We'll need more money.

MAUD. I told Christy that in the telegram. I told him to wire it.

JOHN. He'll need the name o' the bank we've been usin'.

MAUD. I gave it to him.

JOHN. *(Annoyed at her efficiency.)*... Four. Change the plane reservations.

MAUD. Done.

JOHN. And the connecting flight.

MAUD. Done.

JOHN. Call the adoption agency –

MAUD. Done.

JOHN. The car rental place –

MAUD. Done.

JOHN. And the diaper service.

MAUD. Done.

JOHN. *(Slapping the table.) The woman is impossible!*

MAUD. Is there anything else?

JOHN. I could use my toothbrush.

MAUD. Here it is. *(She pulls it out of her purse and gives it to him.)* Now according to the doctor, I get four more minutes today. Would you like to see Miranda?

JOHN. Four minutes?! Get her in here!

MAUD. I'll be right back.

(MAUD EXITS.)

JOHN. I knew that woman would be trouble from the minute I set eyes on her.

MAUD. *(Reentering, with MIRANDA in her arms) Guess* who's here?

JOHN. Let's see her, let's see her....Oh my God, she's gotten cuter!

MAUD. I know.

JOHN. Sweetie-pie, just look at you, you're gettin' bigger every day...

MAUD. *(Pulling out a package.)* She brought you a get-well present.

JOHN. She didn't! The little scamp. *(To the baby.)* I didn't even know you had an allowance. Can you help me open it? Here. Pull on this. Pull. Oh, I'll do it, you good girl you... *(It's a record. He laughs.)* Elvis! Great! And it's got the hound dog on it! That's a wonder. Thanks. I love it. *(To the baby.)* Thank you, sweetie.

MAUD. ... Well?

JOHN. What?

MAUD. How do you plan to play it?

JOHN. I wasn't goin' to bring that up. One o' these days, I'll get a record phonograph.

MAUD. You have one.

JOHN. ...Sorry?

MAUD. You have one. Here. It's a portable. One of those new jobs. *(She lifts it onto the bed.)* Miranda got you that too. Apparently, she had some savings.

JOHN. You're impossible. This costs a fortune!

MAUD. You just plug it in and off it goes. Apparently, teen-age girls go wild for these things. They had one in hot pink.

JOHN. You know money doesn't grow on trees. I could have waited for this.

MAUD. What a good idea. You could have just looked at the record. Then, as you approach Saint Peter some day, with the trumpets of God sounding in your ears, you could say, "Ach. Maybe I should find out what this funny round thing does. *Or is it too late?!"* Uh oh. Time to go.

JOHN. Oh, no! You just got here!

MAUD. Doctor's orders. We'll see you tomorrow.

JOHN. *(He kisses the baby.)* Good-bye, sweetie-pie. Be a good girl.

(MAUD takes the baby. Then she hands JOHN a book.)

MAUD. Oh by the way, I stumbled across this in a book-shop. It's a biography of that poet of yours. Robert Burns.

JOHN. I don't believe it.

MAUD. You need something to read.

JOHN. Jesus Christ. Are you made o' money?!

MAUD. Now you can turn on Elvis and read about Robert Burns at the same time. You'll think you've gone to heaven. I'm sure it's the only way you'll ever get there. We'll see you tomorrow.

(MAUD EXITS with the baby.)

JOHN. Thanks!

(Pause. JOHN looks at the book. Opens it. He shakes his head with disapproval. Thinks. Then he pulls down his covers and slowly gets out of bed. It's a bit of a struggle because his muscles are weak. He kneels by the side of the bed.)

JOHN. Dear Lord. You've put me through quite a lot in one lifetime. I'm not blamin' you, I'm just remindin' you. Now how about givin' me a few more years so I can see what happens to that little girl. *(Pause)* Also, the big spender. Amen.

(The lights fade. Then the lights come up on the house in Scotland and the nurse's station at the hospital. CHRISTY and the nurse are talking on the phone.)

NURSE. But this is the *nurse's station.*

CHRISTY. Yes, I understand that, but could you please put him on the phone. Just this once.

NURSE. It's entirely against the rules. I told you that.

CHRISTY. I understand! But there's no phone in Mr. Campbell's room, and I'm calling from the United Kingdom! All right?

NURSE. Fine! I'll see if I can locate him. *(She puts down the phone.)* The over-sexed old goat..

CHRISTY. Oversexed what...?

(The NURSE throws the covers off JOHN.)

NURSE. You've got a call at the nurses' station. Come

with me.

JOHN. You woke me up!

NURSE. Well, *I* didn't *place* the call, now did I?...

JOHN. I thought I was dead...

NURSE. Come on! Don't dawdle! Calls cost money, you know.

JOHN. Yes sir, Captain Bligh.

NURSE. Why you would get a call from *Disneyland* I have no idea.

JOHN. Disneyland? That's very strange.

NURSE. And you're not, I suppose.

JOHN. *(Into the phone.)* Hello?

CHRISTY. John?

JOHN. Christy. What the hell are you doin' in California?!

CHRISTY. I'm not. I'm here at home.

JOHN. The nurse said you were in Disneyland.

CHRISTY. Disneyland?

JOHN. *(To the NURSE.)* He says he's callin' from Scotland.

NURSE. He said the Magic Kingdom.

CHRISTY. I said the United Kingdom. She must be deaf.

JOHN. She's beyond deaf. She's supernatural.

CHRISTY. Well how the hell are you?

JOHN. I'm getting there I suppose.

CHRISTY. You sound depressed.

JOHN. So would you be if you had this nurse.

CHRISTY. How's the baby?

JOHN. She knows how to wave. At her age. Honest to God.

CHRISTY. Wow.

JOHN. Are you all right?

CHRISTY. I'm fine. I was just ...worried about you.

JOHN. How's Gloria?

CHRISTY. She's great. She's...back to her old self. I'd put her on, but she's out right now.

JOHN. Right. *(Beat; he looks at his watch.)* It's midnight there.

CHRISTY. She'll be back soon. She's out with a friend.

JOHN. Who?

CHRISTY. You don't know him. It's her cousin Henry. One of her hundred and fifty cousins.

(The NURSE walks by and clicks her tongue.)

JOHN. Uh oh. I've got to go. I'm gettin' the evil eye over here from the Queen of Mordor.

CHRISTY. John. Do you need anything?

JOHN. No. We're fine. Thanks.

CHRISTY. Okay. I just...wanted to say hi.

JOHN. Take care of yourself, lad.

CHRISTY. You too.

(They hang up. JOHN looks at the phone, concerned. The lights fade. They come up on the living room of the hotel suite. MAUD is writing a note. She's dressed to go out. The baby is in her carriage, nearby. MAUD finishes the note and puts it on the floor outside JOHN'S room.)

MAUD. All right Miranda, we're going to write Uncle John a little note, then if he wakes up while we're out, he won't get worried.

(MAUD straightens her scarf; then she wheels the baby out the

front door. After a beat, JOHN ENTERS from his room, pulling on his bathrobe. His hair is disheveled and he yawns. He's just up from a nap. He sees the note on the floor and reads it.)

JOHN. Thanks a lot.

(He notices a book on the table — the book of Burns poetry that he gave to MAUD. He gets an idea. He turns on the record player that she bought him, places the needle on the record ... and we hear Elvis singing "You Ain't Nothing' But A Hound Dog." JOHN sits in the armchair, picks up the book and starts to read aloud:)

JOHN. *(Along with "Hound Dog")*
Ye Banks and Braes, by Robert Burns.
"Ye banks and braes o' bonnie Doon,
 How can ye bloom sae fresh and fair?
 How can ye chant, ye little birds,
 And I sae weary fu' o' care?"

The old bat was right. It's heaven.

"Thou'lt break my heart, thou warbling bird,
 That wanders thro' the flowering thorn:
 Thou minds me o' departed joys,
 Departed never to return."

(We hear the "I Love Lucy" theme song — then see CHRISTY and GLORIA sitting in separate chairs in front of the television. The theme song — and then the show — continue under the following:)

GLORIA. I don't even like the name Miranda.

CHRISTY. So we can change it when she gets here. That's not the point. It's the new American show. You'll like it.

GLORIA. You're right, that's not the point, because she should have been here by this time! Upstairs. With her dusty toys. In the nursery. Which I have decorated till I'm blue in the face.

CHRISTY. Gloria, the man had a heart attack!

GLORIA. I know that and I'm sorry. All right? But Maud should get on a plane and bring the baby!

CHRISTY. She doesn't want to! You spoke with her.

GLORIA. I don't care what she wants! It's not her baby, it's mine! ... And the baby would be here by now if you'd let me go in the first place like I asked you to!

(Laughter from the television.)

CHRISTY. Don't call her "the baby." Her name's Miranda.

GLORIA. Not for long. *(A door bell rings.)* That'll be Henry.

CHRISTY. Not again?! You saw him last night.

GLORIA. I am not "seeing" him. He's my cousin. How many times do I have to tell you that? He feels sorry for me. He thinks I'm cooped up.

CHRISTY. *He* thinks so...

GLORIA. We both think so. We're going to a film. That's all. A film!

CHRISTY. Right.

GLORIA. So I'll see you later.

CHRISTY. Right.

GLORIA. ...I won't be late, I promise.

(She hesitates...then kisses him on the head and leaves. We hear more hilarity on the TV, as the scene shifts back to the hotel room in San Francisco.)

MAUD. You're up.

JOHN. In a manner of speakin'.

MAUD. You can put the packages right here, Dimitri.

DIMITRI. Yes, ma'am. *(Whispering, concerned.)* How is Mr. Camp-bell?

MAUD. He's doing much, much better. Here. *(A tip.)*

(DIMITRI waves shyly at JOHN, who waves back. DIMITRI EXITS.)

MAUD. *(Emptying the packages.)* I have to tell you, Miranda is a real party girl. She loves going out. She googled the entire way. Now guess what. I brought a surprise for dinner. I can't even look at room service anymore, so I bought us two "submarines." I thought we'd have a picnic here in the room.

JOHN. What the hell is a "submarine?"

MAUD. *(Taking them out of the bag and unwrapping one of them.)* It's a sort of Italian laxative. That's what the man said. I think he was kidding me. I'm simply dying to try one. They cut a roll in half and put in salad and meat and onions and peppers and oil and anything else they can think of. *(Displaying it.)* There.

JOHN. I don't like onions.

MAUD. You can scrape them off. We picked them up at this darling little hole in the wall called "Tony and Joe's." Tony made them himself. It was like watching Salvador Dali paint The Last Supper with salami. Except Tony has more hair on his chest. I insisted, incidentally, that he wash his hands first. He thought that was a scream. In fact, he took quite a shine to me, so he put in extra cappacola. That's one of the meats. I also bought us something called a "pizza pie."*(She pronounces it "peeza" pie.)* According to Tony, it's the best peeza in San Francisco. Joe agrees with him. They're married, by the way. If you know what I mean. Anyway, Tony says the peeza goes well with the submarine.

JOHN. It's round.

MAUD. It's supposed to be round.

JOHN. It looks like a raccoon was run over with heavy machinery.

MAUD. Try it, it smells luscious.

JOHN. I need a fork.

MAUD. You pick it up with your hands. Like this. Mmm!

JOHN. You're puttin' me on.

MAUD. No, it's a finger food.

JOHN. I like cutlery.

MAUD. Try it this way.

JOHN. I don't want to.

MAUD. Oh, try it anyway.

JOHN. *I don't want to!*

MAUD. Well fine. I'll give you a fork!

JOHN. Don't bother! I'm not eatin' it in any case! I don't like it!

MAUD. How do you know without trying it?!

JOHN. *I can tell by lookin' at it!*

MAUD. *(Through gritted teeth.)*...Would you please... just...try it.

JOHN. *Fine! (He tastes a tiny corner.)* I don't like it.

MAUD. You barely tasted it!

JOHN. I hate it!

MAUD. Then eat the submarine!

JOHN. I don't like that either!

MAUD. You didn't try the submarine!

JOHN. *Well I was right about the peeza wasn't I?!! Christ! I know what I like — I'm a grown man — and I don't like this awful shite for food!!...You treat me like a child! A baby! And I'm supposed to be carin' for a baby! The "lean and slippered pantaloon" — feedin' her bottles! So what the hell am I doin' here?!!*

(Pause.)

MAUD. ...You"re not in a bad mood by any chance...

JOHN. No!

MAUD. Oh. I see.

(She fusses with the baby to keep from looking at him.)

JOHN. ... I am just so sick of bein' cooped up. And feelin' tired all the time. And useless. It makes me feel old. And I'm not old.

MAUD. John. It's called the "recovery period." Of course you feel depressed right now. I've been reading about it. Everyone feels depressed after a major illness. It's common. Even for the Scots.

JOHN. Well I don't like it.

MAUD. Nobody likes it. Do you think people wake up in the morning after a heart attack and say "Oh, goody, goody, I feel like I've been hit by a truck." You should be saying "Thank God it was a mild attack. I'm still alive. Aren't I lucky." It could have been so much worse. You could still be in the hospital. It could be –

JOHN. All right, all right! Stop preachin'. Just forget about it. *(He takes a deep breath.)* Let's start this dinner over. Look, I'm changin' moods. I feel great. Ha, ha. Ho, ho. Just like Karl Marx.

MAUD. Groucho Marx.

JOHN. Right. Now what am I supposed to start with? The ugly red mess with the cheese? Or the laxative – which looks like the biggest suppository in the history of mankind.

MAUD. I believe it's optional.

JOHN. Right. I'll take the mess, you take the "submarine." Whoever's still alive at the end o' the meal can call the funeral undertaker.

(MAUD shakes her head in resignation. They start to eat. The lights fade. The back lawn of the house. CHRISTY is just opening a letter – and there's a picture in it.)

CHRISTY. Gloria! Gloria! Come quick! Look! Look! *(She hurries in.)* It's a picture of Miranda. They sent it last week. Almost a week and a half ago…Oh my God, she's beautiful.

GLORIA. *(Gazing at the picture in surprise.)* She's adorable.

CHRISTY. She has your eyes. They're the spittin' image.

GLORIA. That's ridiculous. She's Celia's baby.

CHRISTY. And you're Celia's cousin.

GLORIA. Well that's true...She doesn't have my mouth, though.

CHRISTY. But she will. Kids take on their parents' expressions. I read about it. So she'll look like me, too, eventually.

GLORIA. Do you think so?

CHRISTY. Absolutely.

GLORIA. ...She won't have to shave, will she?

CHRISTY. Comedian.

GLORIA. What about the chest hair?

CHRISTY. Gloria.

GLORIA. And the beady eyes?

CHRISTY. I'm warning you.

GLORIA. And the big feet, and the ingrown toenail, and the hairy arms, and the lousy tennis game —

(Overlapping)

CHRISTY. Stop it, stop it, stop it. *(They laugh and kiss.)* Let's go out and celebrate.

GLORIA. Really?

CHRISTY. Yeah. Once Miranda gets here we won't get out much.

GLORIA. Don't say that.

CHRISTY. Well not *as* much anyway.

GLORIA. But some.

CHRISTY. Some. We compromise. That's the ticket. Right?

GLORIA. Right.

CHRISTY. I'll go get dressed.

(He kisses her and hurries off. She looks at the picture.
The scene changes to the living room, shrouded in darkness. A
*   door opens, and MAUD ENTERS quietly in her nightgown.*
*   She turns on a table lamp and tiptoes over to the bassinet*
*   and peeks in.)*

MAUD. *(Quietly)* Oh what are you doing with your eyes
open? It's two in the morning!

THE BABY. WHA!

MAUD. Shhh! Did I wake you up? I didn't mean to. *(The*
baby gurgles, and MAUD picks her up.) Would you like a bottle? I prepared it for you, just in case. *(She sits with the baby*
on her lap and produces the bottle.) Wait wait wait, I have to
take the cap off!...There....I thought so. *(She watches the baby*
slurping her bottle.) You are allowed to breathe, you know.
You don't get penalized. *(Pause. The following is said very*
matter-of-factly. It's not maudlin or self-pitying at all.) Hello,
friend. I've never had such a good friend before. *(Beat)* Except
for Jack. You would have liked him. He was very gentle. And
funny. I wish he was here to see you. *(Beat)* I like talking about
him. Otherwise, he fades away, and I can't see him any more.
Your Uncle John taught me that. Isn't it nice having John back?
We missed him terribly, didn't we. So. Tomorrow's the big day.
We go to court and get you a little piece of paper that says we
can take you out of the country. Then we get on a plane — you
won't like that very much, believe me. But we'll keep our eyes
closed. Then it's back to Scotland, where you'll meet your parents. I'm sure you'll like them very much. They're very nice.
And you know I'll still be with you when they let me ... which
should be fairly...*(Her eyes glaze over; she can't finish.)* Oh
look at you. You're falling asleep. Shhh. Close your eyes. Shall

I sing you a song? Would you like that? Shhh.
(Sings quietly.)
"OH, DEAR, WHAT CAN THE MATTER BE,
 DEAR, DEAR, WHAT CAN THE MATTER BE,
 OH, DEAR, WHAT CAN THE MATTER BE,
 JOHNNY'S SO LONG AT THE FAIR."

*(She hugs the baby close to her chest. As she sings the second
    verse, we see JOHN standing in the doorway of his bed-
    room, watching her. We can't quite tell how long he's been
    there, or how much he's heard. As she continues, the lights
    fade.)*

MAUD.
"HE PROMISED HE'D BRING ME A BASKET OF POSIES,
A GARLAND OF LILIES, A GARLAND OF ROSES,
HE PROMISED TO BUY ME A BUNCH OF BLUE RIBBONS
TO TIE UP MY BONNIE BROWN HAIR."

*(The lights are out. Then the air is split by the banging of a
    gavel – and the lights come up inside a courtroom. JUDGE
    LEONARD WEEMS is on the bench, opening the day's ses-
    sion. He's been a judge for 25 years and is instantly intimi-
    dating. He is all facts and hard as nails.)*

JUDGE WEEMS. The Municipal Court, Family Division,
of the County of San Francisco in the State of California is now
in session. The petition before the court is entitled In Re Jane
Doe, Docket Number 55 dash 2081. Now this is an application
for interim adoption, is that correct, counselor?

*(The attorney representing the agency, NANCY BRENNEMAN,
    steps forward. She's a youngish attorney, fairly new to all
    this. Beside her, at a table, sit JOHN and MAUD, wearing
    their Sunday best. The baby is with them, in her bassinet.)*

MISS BRENNEMAN. Yes, your Honor.

JUDGE WEEMS. With a request that the child be permit-
ted to travel outside this jurisdiction and beyond the borders of
the United States.

MISS BRENNEMAN. Yes, your Honor.

JUDGE WEEMS. And the adoptive parents are currently
residing in...Loch Mull, Scotland.

MISS BRENNEMAN. That's correct, your Honor.

JUDGE WEEMS. *(Amused)* And how many people live in
Loch Mull, Scotland?

MISS BRENNEMAN. I really don't know, your Honor.

JOHN. Forty-two. But Mrs. McHenry is expectin' twins in
December.

JUDGE WEEMS. *(Peering over his glasses.)* And you are
...?

JOHN. John Campbell, your Honor. And this is Miss Maud
Kinch.

JUDGE WEEMS. The protocol, Mr. Campbell, is to rise
when you address the bench.

JOHN. *(Standing)* Right. Sorry, your Honor.

(He sits.)

JUDGE WEEMS. Mr. Campbell?
JOHN. Aye?
JUDGE WEEMS. Up.

JOHN. Oh. Sorry.

(He stands again.)

JUDGE WEEMS. Now the two of you plan to escort this child to "Loch Mull." Is that correct?

JOHN. Aye.

JUDGE WEEMS. And does this journey worry you in any way? In terms of caring for the infant?

JOHN. No, sir. Not at all.

JUDGE WEEMS. I understand, Mr. Campbell, that you had a...medical problem recently.

JOHN. Yes, sir, but I'm completely recovered now.

JUDGE WEEMS. Completely?

JOHN. Aye. I've never felt better.

JUDGE WEEMS. Never? In your entire life? You never felt better.

JOHN. ...Well, I —

JUDGE WEEMS. When you were twenty years old. Did you feel better then?

JOHN. I suppose I did. Yes.

JUDGE WEEMS. So your statement to the court was not really accurate, was it, Mr. Campbell.

JOHN. No, sir. I guess not.

JUDGE WEEMS. I guess not. *(Beat)* But you have no qualms about this journey. Either of you.

JOHN. No, sir.

JUDGE WEEMS. Miss Kinch?

MAUD. No, sir.

JUDGE WEEMS. Have you ever had any children? Of your own?

MAUD. No, your honor.

JUDGE WEEMS. Mr. Campbell?

JOHN. I believe that's irrelevant, your Honor.

JUDGE WEEMS. *(Dangerously)* "Irrelevant?" Did I hear you say "irrelevant?"

JOHN. Yes, sir.

JUDGE WEEMS. In what sense would you call it "irrelevant," Mr. Campbell?

JOHN. In the sense that it's not worth talkin' about. I know how to take care of the child — !

JUDGE WEEMS. Mr. Campbell! In my courtroom, I decide what is relevant and what is not relevant. Is that clear?!

JOHN. ... Aye.

JUDGE WEEMS. Then perhaps you'd be good enough to answer my question. Do you have any children?

JOHN. No, sir!

JUDGE WEEMS. Thank you.

(The JUDGE, annoyed, returns to his papers. Then:)

JOHN. ...Not now. *(Beat)* I had a son, but when he was two years old, he and his mother died in the influenza epidemic.

MAUD. *(Standing)* John...

JUDGE WEEMS. I see. I'm sorry to hear that. It is, however, relevant. Now Miss Brenneman, I see here that we have a social work profile of the adoptive parents, a Christy and Gloria McCall," performed at "Loch Mull" just three weeks ago by a local Scottish agency. However, I see no social worker's report on Mr. Campbell and Miss Kinch. Why is that?

MISS BRENNEMAN. I ... I don't know, your Honor. I suppose I ... didn't think it was necessary to order it.

JUDGE WEEMS. And yet this child will be traveling six thousand miles beyond our jurisdiction with two complete strangers to this court.

MISS BRENNEMAN. I ...suppose that's true, your Honor, but I —

JUDGE WEEMS. We are responsible for this child, counselor. She is our sacred trust.

MISS BRENNEMAN. I see that, your Honor, but —

JUDGE WEEMS. I'm afraid that I'm inclined, under the circumstances, to order a stay of one week on the current application, or until such time as a profile can be prepared on Mr. Campbell and Miss Kinch. Until that time, since this court has no knowledge as to whether these two people can take care of a child, the baby shall be returned to the foster home —

JOHN. Your Honor!

MAUD. Oh, no!

JUDGE WEEMS. — where she resided for the first two weeks of her life. *(He bangs his gavel.)* So ordered.

JOHN. Your Honor, can I say somethin'.

JUDGE WEEMS. No.

JOHN. *(Very angry.) Your Honor, please.*

(Pause.)

JUDGE WEEMS. ...Make it brief.

JOHN. ...Your Honor, if I understand you correctly, you want to make certain that Miss Kinch and I can take care o' this child and get her safely to her new parents.

JUDGE WEEMS. Something like that, yes.

JOHN. Your Honor, we have been carin' for Miranda for almost five weeks now.

JUDGE WEEMS. That was an oversight, and the agency will be hearing from this court.

JOHN. Whatever it was, your Honor, have you ever seen a happier child in your whole life? Look for yourself. Look! Now what can a social worker tell you that you cannot see with your own eyes? Here we are, standin' in front of you. I suspect you could ask us better questions and make a better judgment for yourself than somebody who the state or the county or whatever would be sendin' to see us some time in the future.

JUDGE WEEMS. I'm sorry, I have a very busy schedule, Mr. Campbell.

JOHN. And for that you're goin' to disrupt this child's life?! She's had enough disruptions as it is. Your Honor, I can promise you there are no two people on this planet that could ever love this child more than we do. I would gladly walk in front of a freight train to save her life without a second thought.

MAUD. I feel exactly the same way, your Honor.

(During the following, MIRANDA starts crying – and her crying gets louder and louder as JUDGE WEEMS, who has to keep raising his voice, continues:)

JUDGE WEEMS. ... Mr. Campbell. Miss Kinch. The fact of the matter is that you are both strangers to this court; that this child is under the jurisdiction of this court, which is entrusted, by law, to ensure that she remains unharmed and well cared for; and furthermore, we have no evidence whatsoever that either of you has any genuine experience in how to care for this child or any other child ...

(By this time JOHN and MAUD are attending to MIRANDA.)

MAUD. I think she's hungry.

JOHN. I have a bottle right here.

MAUD. There, there, sweetheart. You'll be fine.

JOHN. Shh. That's right. It's Uncle John. You're doin' okay…

MAUD. That's our girl. Oh. I'm sorry, your honor.

JOHN. Sorry.

MAUD. You were saying?

(The JUDGE eyes them unhappily.)

JUDGE WEEMS. Have the two of you ever heard the expression "pain in the butt?"

JOHN. Yes, sir.

MAUD. Yes sir.

JUDGE WEEMS. I will see both of you in my chambers at noon. And be prepared, Mr. Campbell, to be grilled like a chicken. *(He bangs his gavel.)* Court adjourned!

(MAUD and JOHN embrace with relief. The lights instantly brighten and we're on a trendy street in San Francisco, outside a trendy restaurant. We hear the sounds of a restaurant: murmuring voices, laughter, and the clink of plates and glasses.)

JOHN. I'm not sure I like the neighborhood.

MAUD. Oh *I* do! It'll be an adventure! And what an unusual restaurant.

JOHN. Would you rather go elsewhere?

MAUD. No, no. It looks like fun.

(At this moment, a TRENDY WAITER glides to the table on a pair of roller skates. His hair is henna'd bright red and is in a pony tail. He wears an oversized bow tie and an earring, and he's carrying two fancy drinks on a tray.)

TRENDY WAITER. Here we are, two mango mint delights to celebrate Bastille Day. *(He serves the drinks singing the first few lines of the Marseillaise:)* "Da da da daa daa daa daa daaaaa da dum." "It is a far, far better thing I drink than I have ever drunk before." Can I tell you our specials for the night? We have ravioli stuffed with spinach and goat cheese, which is better than a goat stuffed with spinach and ravioli. We have mahi-mahi, the fish, not the dance, broiled in a crust of seaweed. And on our you-had-it-here-first menu, we have fresh buffalo steak char-broiled on the open grill and rattle snake sauteed in butter and seasonal herbs. Yum. Give it a think and I'll be back in a flash.

(He circles the table and points to the baby.)

TRENDY WAITER. Oh, cute!

(And he's gone.)

MAUD. … I'm going to miss California.
JOHN. It sort o' makes redundant the whole notion o' space travel.
MAUD. Well, cheers.
JOHN. Cheers. Here's to some very happy memories of the American continent.
MAUD. Here, here.

(They clink their glasses and taste their drinks.)

JOHN. While we're at it, you might as well open this.

(He pulls out a present for MAUD. It's a small package, gift-wrapped.)

MAUD. What's that?

JOHN. It looks suspiciously like a present to me.

MAUD. *(Opening the package.)* Oh...I'll bet it's a pair of gloves, isn't it. You're making fun of me. Well, as it happens, I *need* gloves, so there.

JOHN. It occurred to me this mornin' that our entire relationship is defined by expensive presents. This is quite unusual for a Scotsman.

(The present is open, but it's not a pair of gloves, it's two small folders.)

MAUD. Tickets? I don't understand. What's "Holland-American?"

JOHN. It's a boat company. We still have to fly to New York, but we're sailin' back home the rest of the way. It's sort of a...cruise ship sort o' thing. I know you don't like to fly, so —

MAUD. ...John!

JOHN. I wanted to say thank you for takin' such good care of me. While I was sick.

MAUD. Oh, John, you're such a dear! But what about Gloria? And Christy? They'll be so upset.

JOHN. No. I rang 'em this morning. I told 'em there was an airline strike and it was the boat or nothin'.

MAUD. John! You scoundrel!

JOHN. I'm sore ashamed, but you deserve it in spades. *(He smiles conspiratorially.)* On top of which, it gives us another week with Miranda.

MAUD. It does, doesn't it. *(She clutches the tickets to her bosom.)* Ohh, I can't wait!...Look. She's asleep again.

(They look at her in awe.)

JOHN. It's no wonder she always looks so beautiful. *I'd* look good if I slept sixteen hours a day.

MAUD. You do sleep sixteen hours a day.

JOHN. Thanks a lot.

(At which point, the TRENDY WAITER skates up to the table.)

TRENDY WAITER. What are you two doing?! Look at those drinks. You've barely touched them. That's it. Two more drinks on the house. I want you two to get very drunk by the end of the evening. Now – have you decided yet about the meal?

MAUD. How's the buffalo tonight?

TRENDY WAITER. To be honest, it's a little chewy.

MAUD. Then I'll have the rattle snake.

JOHN. Make that two. *(Beat)* If we die, we die.

(As the WAITER collects their menus and zooms off, the lights fade. They then come up on the house in Scotland. Glo-

ria's bedroom. There's an open suitcase on the bed, and GLORIA is methodically packing her clothes. CHRISTY is sitting nearby. They're both upset and emotionally fragile. Silence, as GLORIA continues to pack. Then:)

CHRISTY. I just...I can't believe it.
GLORIA. I'm sorry.
CHRISTY. Our anniversary is next week.
GLORIA. I said I'm sorry!

(She almost breaks down...but controls herself and goes back to packing.)

CHRISTY. Are you in love with Henry?
GLORIA. I don't know.
CHRISTY. I know that you slept with him.

(GLORIA stiffens unconsciously.)

GLORIA. Who told you that?
CHRISTY. I can just tell....It doesn't mean you have to leave.
GLORIA. That's not why I'm leaving.
CHRISTY. What about the baby? *(No response.)* Gloria? What about the baby?
GLORIA. I don't know.
CHRISTY. That's not good enough.
GLORIA. *I don't know! What do you want me to say?! I don't know everything! I'm sorry! I don't know what to do!!*

(She breaks into sobs. CHRISTY holds her, and she sobs on his shoulder.)

CHRISTY. Hey. Hey hey hey. Come on, now. I love you. And you love me. That's all that matters. Right?

GLORIA. *(Crying)* I don't know!

CHRISTY. Look …*(CHRISTY makes a decision.)* we can live in London. Would you like that?

GLORIA. Oh Christy, I'm so sorry, I'm so very…it's just… I never knew what things would be like here, I mean, I thought I did but after I was sick…I'm so ashamed. I'm *so* sorry!

CHRISTY. Hey. What's your favorite thing to do in the whole world? Just name it. Your favorite favorite. *(Beat. Then GLORIA giggles through her tears.)* Besides that. In addition to that.

GLORIA. That.

CHRISTY. Now?

GLORIA. That.

CHRISTY. I'll close the door.

GLORIA. No. Leave it open.

CHRISTY. The maid is down the hall.

GLORIA. Too bad.

CHRISTY. Gloria!

(She starts to climb all over him and they fall down onto the bed.)

GLORIA. That that that that that that that that that that …. CHRISTY. Gloria!

(As they start to make love, the lights fade. In the darkness, we

hear the deep hoot of an ocean liner sounding its horn. The lights come up on JOHN, leaning on the rail of the ship, looking out to sea. The night sky is filled with stars. After a pause, he begins reciting to himself.)

JOHN.
"Go fetch to me a pint o' wine,
An' fill it in a silver tassie;
That I may drink, before I go,
A service to my bonnie lassie.

That boat rocks at the pier o' Leith,
Fu' loud the wind blaws frae the ferry,
The ship rides by the Berwick-law,
And I maun leave my bonnie Mary."

(About now, MAUD APPEARS and he recites the rest to her.)

"The trumpets sound, the banners fly,
The glittering spears are rankéd ready;
The shouts o' war are heard afar,
The battle closes thick deep and bloody;
But it's no the roar o' sea or shore
Wad mak me langer with to tarry;
Nor shout o' war that's heard afar,
It's leaving thee, my bonnie Mary."

Where's Miranda?

MAUD. She's at the Captain's table. The Captain's wife swears that Miranda is the most beautiful child she's ever seen.

JOHN. I liked that woman from the moment I set eyes on her.

(They lean on the rail and look out to sea. The mood changes. Then:)

MAUD. One more day to go.
JOHN. Aye.
MAUD. Then we hand her over.
JOHN. We do.

(Pause.)

MAUD. ...Do you think they'll let us...feed her now and then? Change her?

JOHN. I don't know why not. But she'll be their child from tomorrow on. It'll be up to them.

MAUD. Of course it will. And it's not as if we won't see her. All the time. Unless they travel, I suppose...Or move away ...They've got to make their own life. They should. It's their child. It's not...

(She breaks down completely. She sobs uncontrollably. JOHN holds her.)

MAUD. John...I don't think I can bear giving her up.
JOHN. Shhh.
MAUD. John ?
JOHN. Yes?
MAUD. *(Fiercely)* What if *we* adopted her. You and I. They

haven't even met her yet. They don't even know her! They're young! They can find another child! They have time! I know it's selfish. I know it! But I can't help it! I've thought about nothing else for days and days. *(No answer.)* ...John?

JOHN. ...I've been thinkin' exactly the same thing.

MAUD. Oh, John.

JOHN. But there's one big problem. There isn't a court in Scotland that'd let us adopt Miranda unless we were married. It'll be the law.

MAUD. Do you really think so?

JOHN. I'm positive.

(Long pause.)

JOHN. So what the hell are we waitin' for?

(The ship's horn blows and the lights fade. The lights come up on another part of the deck, a day later, as the ship is docking at Southampton. We hear the noises of the arrival: horns, scurrying people, reunions. JOHN and MAUD EN-TER pushing the carriage.)

CHRISTY. *(Off)* John! Maud! Over here!

MAUD. Look. There they are. Are you ready?

JOHN. I think so.

MAUD. Are you going to tell them or should I?

JOHN. I don't think I can do it. It'll break his heart.

MAUD. I'll do it then.

(CHRISTY and GLORIA ENTER happily.)

CHRISTY. There they are! *John!*
GLORIA. *Aunt Maud!*
CHRISTY. *John! Over here!*
GLORIA. I can't believe we're doing this.
CHRISTY. It'll be fine, I promise.

(By now, JOHN and MAUD have joined them and they all embrace.)

JOHN. Hello, lad! You're lookin' well.
CHRISTY. Look at you! You look fine!
MAUD. Gloria, dear. You look wonderful. And so happy.
GLORIA. I *am* happy. I'm so happy. Oh, Aunt Maud...
(She looks into the carriage.) I guess that's her.
JOHN. That's herself.
CHRISTY. Wow.
GLORIA. Just look at her. She's so beautiful. *(She stares in awe.)* Oh my God...

(MAUD glances at JOHN. She takes the plunge.)

MAUD. Gloria. *(Pause. No response.)* Gloria.
GLORIA. Yes, Aunt Maud?
MAUD. Now listen. It's about the baby...
CHRISTY. *(Quickly)* Is she all right?!
MAUD. She's fine, just fine.
CHRISTY. You scared me.
MAUD. She's in perfect health. She couldn't be better. But I need to...there's something that I have to...say, because...

(She can't do it.)

GLORIA. What is it?

MAUD. It's just that…

GLORIA. *What?!*

MAUD. …I think you should hold your baby.

(Beat. MAUD turns away.)

GLORIA. Aunt Maud…I have to tell you something, and you're not going to be happy about it. *(Beat)* Christy and I have been having some…

CHRISTY. Marital difficulties –

GLORIA. And we've been trying hard to work them out. I'm sure it's all my fault –

CHRISTY. Gloria –

GLORIA. It *is*. I mean, I'm just not made to live in a small town. I need adventures, and things to *do*, and…about a month ago, I started seeing my cousin Henry. Socially.

MAUD. Henry?

GLORIA. I only confused things more. I've come to realize that I'm…just not ready –

CHRISTY. *We're* not ready.

GLORIA. *We're* not ready…emotionally, I mean…to take care of a baby. We still need time to have friends, and live in London –

CHRISTY. Just part of the time –

GLORIA. And *do* things. Because our marriage can still work – I know it can! But we just can't do it right now if we *have* a baby. So…

CHRISTY. We feel terrible about this, but –

GLORIA. We've decided that …

CHRISTY. We'll have to put the baby up for adoption.

GLORIA. Or find her a home somewhere –

CHRISTY. with some friends.

GLORIA. At least at her age she won't know the difference.

CHRISTY. That'll be all right, don't you think? John?

GLORIA. Aunt Maud?

(By this time, all JOHN and MAUD can do is gaze at each other in speechless joy.)

JOHN. Come here, woman.

(They give a whoop of delight and MAUD jumps into JOHN'S arms. They crow with joy and kiss lustily.)

GLORIA. Aunt Maud!

CHRISTY. John!

(And now bagpipes are playing. The lights change and we're in the church at Loch Mull, near the pulpit. We hear the murmur of the congregation. The stage is empty for a moment. Then the bagpipers strike up "Here Comes The Bride." MAUD appears holding CHRISTY'S arm, and they march down the aisle. MAUD looks radiant. When they reach the pulpit, CHRISTY hands MAUD over to JOHN as groom. Then GLORIA hands MIRANDA to MAUD. PARSON Mc-NAIR steps behind the pulpit, and the ceremony begins.)

PARSON McNAIR. Dearly beloved. We are gathered here in the sight o' God to join in holy matrimony Mr. John Campbell and Miss Maud Kinch. For those of us who have known John for most of our lives, we have one thing to say: It's about time. For those of us who have gotten to know Miss Maud Kinch over the past year or so, we say that John here is a lucky man. And for those of us who have met Miranda in the past few days, we say that John and Maud are a lucky couple ... and we thank 'em both for increasin' the population o' Loch Mull.

(JOHN leans over and kisses MAUD.)

PARSON McNAIR. Nay, wait for that stuff 'til we're finished! Ya sex maniac. *(Shakes his head.)* I could a' told ya that *forty* years ago...*(Then it's back to the ceremony.)* Now I'm goin' to begin with a bit o' scripture, so sit back and listen, you might learn somethin'. It's from the Book o' Ruth. Or maybe it's Samuel, I get 'em mixed up. Just listen.

(As he begins the scripture, the lights fade slowly on everything but JOHN, MAUD and MIRANDA, who end up in a bright, white light. Meanwhile, we hear "Be My Baby," the heavenly harmonized voices at the beginning of the song. As the PARSON speaks, JOHN and MAUD kiss.)

PARSON McNAIR. *(Orating grandly.)* "Entreat me not to leave thee, or to return from followin' after thee: for whither thou goest, I will go; and where thou lodgest, I will lodge: thy people shall be my people, and thy God my God. Where thou diest, will I die, and there will I be buried: the Lord do so to me, and more also, if ought but death part thee and me..."

CURTAIN

PROPERTY PLOT

JOHN - Personal
Scotland Coat
Dirty Cloth
Plane Tickets – in overcoat
Shopping List –Brown Jacket
Pad And Pencil –Brown Jacket

MAUD - Personal
Black Purse- Act 1
      Coin Purse
      Kleenex

Beige Purse-Act 2
      Compact
      Kleenex
      Toothbrush
      Room Key # 2
      One-Dollar Bill

MALE ENSEMBLE DRESSING ROOM – Personal
Vintage Pen

PROP TABLE #1 -TOP SHELF

Lint Brush	John
Watch	John
Letter W/ Envelope	Gloria
Envelope With Papers	John
Immigration Papers	John
State Court Petition	John
Health Certificate	John
Birth Certificate	John
Interstate Compact Approval	John
2 Plates Of Sorbet	Maitre D'
2 Streamers	
Photo Of Miranda	Christy
Rob Roy Drinkw/ Cherry, Ice-Airplane	Stewardess
Tray W/ 2 Drinks	Waitress

Waitress Order Pad And Pencil   Waitress
2 Mango Mint Delights W/ Ice Umbrellas   Trendy Waiter

PROP TABLE #1 - 2ND SHELF
Scotland Plaid Throw   Christy
Gloria's Clothes To Pack   Gloria
Stethoscope   Doctor
Newspaper   Passenger
Door Stick

PROP CABINET #1
Room Key #2 *(Preset In John's Costume By Victoria)*
Album Of Elvis # 1: Check For Album   Maud
Portable Record Player # 1   Maud
Book: Biography Of Robert Burns   Maud
Baby   Beverly
Blanket Secured, One Arm Free

OFFSTAGE / ONSTAGE
Wedding Dress   Maud
Sewing Kit   Maud
Thimble With Double Stick Tape
Needle With White Thread
Scissors
Bible   Parson
Flask   Parson
Luggage - Carry On   Maud
Luggage - Carry On   John
Cup Of Water

SR PEW
White Flower Arrangements
Wheelbarrow   Gardener
Cabbage
Beets
2 Turnips
2 Onions
Cloth
2 Cronies (Dead Rabbits)

CAFÉ TABLE
2 Tablecloths
2 Bentwoods
2 Wine Glasses
2 Plates
2 Fancy Folded Napkins
2 Silver Settings
Votive

SOFA
2 Throwpillows
Under (Right)US Throw Pillow
       Baby Bottle   John
       Burping Cloth For Shoulder   John

SOFA TABLE
Small Table Lamp
Radio

ROOM SERVICE CART   Dimitri
Plate With Fake Food   Dimitri
Silver Dome Over Plate
Oatmeal Bowl W/Real Oatmeal
Spoon With The Bowl
1 Coffee Cups/Saucer
Coffee Pot
Creamer And Sugar

TELEVISION SET/EARS DOWN   Christy

SR AIRPLANE SEAT (SINGLE)
Passenger Airplane Blanket
Passenger Airplane Pillow

GLORIA'S BED
Mattress
Sheets
Pillows
Bedskirt
Bedspread
Suitcase
Clothes

BANQUETTE
Table
Long Fern
2 Boat Tickets

ARMCHAIR
Throw Pillow
Side Table
Table Lamp
Telephone

COURTROOM TABLE
3 Chairs
Briefcase With Papers
Click Pen
Folder With Papers

CAR SEAT

KITCHEN TABLE   Ms. Adams
Bowl Of Apples   Ms. Adams
Dough   Ms. Adams
Mixing Bowl
Towel Covering Bowl
Towel On Table
Wooden Spoon
Knife
Pot Of "Haggis"   Maud
Dry Ice & Water (At 5 Mins)
Metal Tongs
Metal Spoon   Ms. Adams
Cutting Board

SL PEW
White Flower Arrangements
Maud's Corsage On White Towel

CHURCH DOORS- KNIFED
4 White Bows
Gloria's Armchair

HOTEL/RESTAURANT DOORS
Bassinette   Maud
Bag Of Purchases   Maud

MAITRE D' PODIUM
Reservation Book   Maitre D'
2 Menus   Maitre D'

PRAM/CARRIAGE   Maud
Baby Bottle With Small Nipple
Speaker Box
1 Blankets
Pillow

JUDGE'S BENCH
Gavel
Folders With Papers
Haight/Ashbury Sign

HOSPITAL BED- BAR PULLED OUT
1 Pillows
1 Blanket
Fitted Sheet
Flat Sheet
Medical Chart   Doctor

HOSPITAL CHAIR

HOSPITAL SCREEN

HOSPITAL SIDE TABLE
Pitcher Of Water   Nurse
Glass Of Water   John
List   John
Kitchen Chair

SL AIRPLANE SEATS (DOUBLE)
Book: Dr. Spock On Baby Care"   John
Newspaper
Pillow Velcro'd To Back Of Seat

PARK BENCH

PROP TABLE #2 -TOP SHELF

Tony & Joe's Paper Bag	Dimitri
Submarine Sandwich	
Tablecloth	
Fork	
2 Napkins	
Pizza Takeout Box	Dimitri

PROP TABLE #2 - SECOND SHELF

Multicolored Bouquet For Bride	Maud
White Bouquet For Bride	Gloria
Maud's Pad And Pencil	
Book	Maud
Note For John (Get From Dixie)	Maud
Blue Vintage Pen	
Ring Of Keys	Dimitri

PROP TABLE #2 - THIRD SHELF

Tea Kettle w/Real Tea
2 Tea Cups With Saucers
Pot Warmer
2 Streamers

PROP CABINET #2 - TOP SHELF

3 Candles	
Book: Double For Burns Poetry	Maud
Portable Record Player # 2	John
Album Of Elvis # 2: "Forever Elvis"	John
Waiter's Tray	
2 Mango Mint Delights	

PROP CABINET #2 - SECOND SHELF

Canvas Grocery Carrier	John
Nightshirt	John
Belt	John
Bottle And Nipple	John
Nappie/Diaper & Pin	John

Mickey Mouse Club Ears	John
Gift: Poetry Book, Wrapped	John
Diaper Bag-	Robin

1 Dirty Diaper
1 Clean Diaper
Pew Decorations/ Multicolored Flowers

CONSUMABLES
Stage Right
3 Rob Roys With False Ice And A Cherry
Toast
Oatmeal
Tea In Coffee Pot

Stage Left
Dough In Bowl
Tea In Tea Kettle
Dry Ice In Tupperware
Hot Water For The Dry Ice
1 Slice Of Pizza

KEN LUDWIG has had a number of hits on Broadway, in the West End of London and throughout the world, including *Lend Me A Tenor, Crazy For You, Moon Over Buffalo, Twentieth Century, Leading Ladies, Be My Baby* and *Shakespeare in Hollywood*, which was commissioned by the Royal Shakespeare Company. His adaptations include *Treasure Island, The Three Musketeers*, and *The Adventures of Tom Sawyer* (a musical). *Crazy For You* won the Tony Award for Best Musical. In addition, he has received the coveted Laurence Olivier Award from the London Society of West End Theatres, as well as two Tony Award nominations, two Helen Hayes Awards, and the Edwin Forrest Award for Contributions to Drama. He studied music at Harvard with Leonard Bernstein and theatre history at Cambridge University in England. Stars who have appeared in the premieres of his plays include Carol Burnett, Lynn Redgrave, Alec Baldwin, Joan Collins, Robert Goulet, Mickey Rooney, Hal Holbrook, Dixie Carter and Frank Langella. (See www.kenludwig.com)

Also by Ken Ludwig...

The Beaux' Stratagem

Crazy for You

Leading Ladies

Lend Me a Tenor

Moon Over Buffalo

Postmortem

Shakespeare in Hollywood

Sullivan & Gilbert

The Adventures of Tom Sawyer

Treasure Island

The Three Musketeers

Twentieth Century

Please visit our website **SAMUELFRENCH.COM** *for complete descriptions and licensing information*

OTHER TITLES AVAILABLE FROM SAMUEL FRENCH

LEADING LADIES

Ken Ludwig

Full Length, Comedy / 5m, 3f / Unit set.

In this hilarious comedy by the author of *Lend Me A Tenor* and *Moon Over Buffalo*, two English Shakespearean actors, Jack and Leo, find themselves so down on their luck that they are performing "Scenes from Shakespeare" on the Moose Lodge circuit in the Amish country of Pennsylvania. When they hear that an old lady in York, PA is about to die and leave her fortune to her two long lost English nephews, they resolve to pass themselves off as her beloved relatives and get the cash. The trouble is, when they get to York, they find out that the relatives aren't nephews, but nieces! Romantic entanglements abound, especially when Leo falls head-over-petticoat in love with the old lady's vivacious niece, Meg, who's engaged to the local minister. Meg knows that there's a wide world out there, but it's not until she meets "Maxine and Stephanie" that she finally gets a taste of it.

"Ken Ludwig is a national treasure. He has almost single-handedly kept alive the sense of humor of Philip Barry, Billy Wilder, Preston Sturgis, George S. Kaufman, and the Marx Brothers. With *Lend Me a Tenor* and *Moon Over Buffalo*, Ludwig established himself as the American playwright to look to for the fast and furious comedic stylings of those masters...Slapstick goofiness, scrambled Shakespeare, and good-natured laughs make *Leading Ladies* an irresistible treat."
– Montana Reperatory Theatre

"Ludwig's newest farce is so funny, it will make sophisticated and reasonable men and women of the 21st century cackle till their faces hurt."
– *Houston Press*

"*Leading Ladies* is consistently funny-indeed, increasingly hilarious as it progresses."
– *Houston Chronicle*

"Look for *Leading Ladies* to become a staple of summer stock and community theatres. And, mind you, I mean that as a compliment."
– *Variety*

SAMUELFRENCH.COM

OTHER TITLES AVAILABLE FROM SAMUEL FRENCH

MOON OVER BUFFALO

Ken Ludwig

Full Length, Comedy / 4m, 4f / Unit set.

Charlotte and George Hay, an acting couple are on tour in Buffalo in 1953 with a repertory consisting of *Cyrano de Bergerac* "revised, one nostril version" and Noel Coward's *Private Lives*. This backstage farce by the author of *Lend Me a Tenor* brought Carol Burnett back to Broadway co-starring with Philip Bosco as her megalomanic, drunken husband and leading man. Fate has given these thespians one more shot at starring roles in *The Scarlet Pimpernel* epic and director Frank Capra himself is en route to Buffalo to catch their matinee performance. Will Charlotte appear or run off with their agent? Will George be sober enough to emote? Will Capra see *Cyrano, Private Lives* or a disturbing mixture of the two? Hilarious misunderstandings pile on madcap misadventures, in this valentine to Theatre Hams everywhere.

"Hilarious ... building up its laughs methodically shtick by shtick.... Ludwig stuffs his play with comic invention, running gags ... and a neat sense of absurdity.... Go and enjoy."
– *The New York Post*

"Somewhere up above ... George S. Kaufman, Abe Burrows, Moss Hart and all those clever fellows who wrote the comedies of yesteryear are rolling with laughter, echoing the audience last night at ... *Moon Over Buffalo*.... The play is nothing less than a love letter to live theater."
– *Boston Herald*

OTHER TITLES AVAILABLE FROM SAMUEL FRENCH

LEND ME A TENOR

Ken Ludwig

Full Length, Comedy-Farce / 4m, 4f / Int.

Nominee! Best Revival of a Play - 2010 Tony® Awards!

This night in September of 1934 is the biggest in the history of the Cleveland Grand Opera Company. World famous tenor Tito Morelli is to perform Otello, his greatest role, at the gala season opener. Saunders, the harried General Manager, hopes this will put Cleveland on the cultural map. Morelli is nowhere to be found; when he finally arrives drunk, it is too late for any rehearsal. Through a hilarious series of mishaps, 'Il Stupendo' is given a double dose of tranquilizers which mix with the booze he has consumed and he passes out. His pulse is so low that Saunders and his assistant Max believe he is dead. What to do? Saunders coaxes Max into Morelli's costume, intending to fool the audience with this fake 'Il Stupendo', blackface and all. Nervous amateur Max succeeds admirably, but Morelli revives and dresses for his second act. With two Otellos now in costume and two women en dishabille, each thinking she is with 'Il Stupendo', the farce spins out of control onstage and off. A sensation on Broadway and in London's West End, *Lend Me a Tenor* is guaranteed to leave your audiences teary eyed with laughter. A new production opened on Broadway during the 2010 season.

> "A jolly play."
> – *The New York Times*

> "Non stop laughter."
> – *Variety*

> "Uproarious! Hysterical!"
> – *USA Today*

> "A rib tickling comedy."
> – *New York Post*